I0778445

JANEEN SWART

A VISIT HOME

By

Janeen Swart

Chapter 1

June 1951: Catherine

Tom and I stop our game of hopscotch when we hear Dad yelling, our feet making footprints in the dark soil between the sidewalk and the building where grass should have been. My eyes widen as I watch him come out of our weathered apartment carrying a huge wooden sign. His face scares me. I stand in awe with a pain beginning deep down in my belly.

Mom yells from inside, "Don't do it, George. We can figure out something."

The banging of the hammer keeps our attention for a moment. Dad finishes and stands back to admire his work. The words make no sense to me, but Mom comes out with tears streaming down her cheeks. Tom and I rush to hug her, but she pushes us aside. "Go play your game."

My shoulders sag. Tom grabs my hand, and we walk back toward the sidewalk. I stand staring at the sign.

"Finish your turn," Tom yells to break my trance.

"Why are our parents always yelling? I want our family to be happy again." Tom shrugs. Hopping along the squares of chalk lines on the sidewalk, tears form in my eyes. My foot slips when I land, and I fall to the side.

"You stepped on the line," calls Tom, laughing.

My legs feel like rubber beneath me. I pull my knees tight to my chest to keep my heart from beating too wildly. People walking by stop to read the sign and point. Dad stalks back toward the apartment door and enters, but Mom seems unable to move.

I look to Tom, but he's oblivious. All he says is, "Let's keep playing. My turn."

Dad comes back out and takes Mom by the arm, yanking her toward the inside of the
apartment. She yells at him to take the sign down, but he screams back, "We've got too many kids. We can't feed them. We need the money. This is the only way."

Jane, my oldest sister, and the other older kids come out to see what all the ruckus is. Jane reads the sign aloud, and her face contorts, trying to hold back tears.

I pull on her arm. "What does it mean?"

"It means it's time to leave this crappy place." She motions to William, next in line in our large family. "Come on let's go." They both turn to walk toward the corner grocery leaving us smaller kids to deal with the scene.

Time stands still while this memory burns into my brain. I watch, wanting it all to stop, as Dad storms off down the street. "Dad, don't go," I yell, but it's no use.

He's already too far away to hear me or doesn't care to hear.

The door slams shut as Mom goes back into the tenement. She comes out with a hammer and works on trying to get the nails pulled from the sign. I try to help but a sliver from the dry wood punctures my finger, and I sit down on the step holding my hand, not wanting to let on that I'm hurt. The emptiness in my chest moves all the way down to my feet, keeping me glued to the spot.

A dark sedan pulls up in front of our building. Its shiny finish contrasts with the drab sidewalk, dirt filled lawn and dark wood siding.

A guy with a news pin on his hat steps out of the car. "Hey, lady, can I get a photo?

Mom turns and hurries toward the apartment door. "You kids, get back in here."

The twins and little Jacob hurry to follow, but I stand up, my body remaining a statue, watching the guy approach. Tom grabs my hand but I'm still unable to move.

The photographer doesn't wait for permission. He gets closer and moves his camera into position. I look down as he snaps the picture, but Tom smiles right into the camera.

Mom shouts at him, "Don't you dare print that."

Her loud voice wakes something inside of me, and I can finally move. I pull Tom toward the building, and we move into the apartment. We plaster our faces up against the grimy window as the man with the camera hops back into his car. The driver steps on the gas to leave our filthy neighborhood.

~

When I catch a glimpse of the photo in the newspaper Mrs. Hopkins, our neighbor, drops onto the table, my eyes feel bound open with glue. Checking the date, June 5, 1951, at the top of the paper, finally allows me to blink. This bizarre photo of Tom and me standing in front of the sign Dad had crudely painted to say, "For Sale, Two Kids," becomes real.

Mom bursts into tears when she reads the headline. I place my arm around the back of her neck, rubbing gently as I ask myself, what will happen if everyone reads this story? My stomach turns like an eggbeater and tears form behind my lids. My siblings gather around Mom and me, their sad faces mirroring mine.

Everything in our small apartment seems to vanish as we all focus on the photo. My vision blurs even more making the scene in the paper run together into a black and white blob. Mom reads the accompanying news story aloud, her voice quavering, stopping often to wipe away a tear. Her neck stiffens more under my touch as she reads. Mrs. Hopkins grabs her newspaper and slips toward the door of the dingy apartment, keeping her eyes averted from our dad.

"Let me see that. They have no right." Dad takes the paper from our neighbor's hands, looks at the photo and throws it onto the floor for Mrs. Hopkins to retrieve.

Our parents scream at each other, their words fly like stinging wasps making welts on my inner spirit. The yelling loses its force somewhat as I run to hide under the bed and cover my ears. The sounds will echo inside my head long after this day. Mary Jane and Johnny, the twins, a year older than me, join me. When Tom snuggles close, I pull him into a bear hug. Soon even my oldest siblings, Jane and William, crawl under from the other side, along with little Jacob who always follows William around.

With no walls in the apartment, two mismatched beds stand side by side, not far from the kitchen area, so the underside of the bed provides little relief from our parents' voices. Silence follows the storm, and Dad plops down at the small kitchen table, head resting in his hands.

Mom whispers, "What are we going to do?" Her soft whimpering fills the space like a lost kitten crying.

Jane says what we're all thinking, her voice raspy, "What if someone actually comes and wants to buy two of us?"

Ever since Dad lost his job when things get tough, he does his usual. He leaves the tiny apartment, slamming the door behind him. This time Mom follows him and yells back behind her. "You're in charge, Jane." The space becomes larger and safer again.

I feel secure enough to come out from under the bed, and the other kids do the same. Jane gathers us together for a group hug. "We've got to stick together."

"I'm hungry," says little Jacob, but there's only a few dry bread slices left on the table from yesterday's dinner. And when Jane tells me to get out the oatmeal, I find it's infested with weevils.

I whine, "Yuk, we can't eat this. What are we going to do for food?"

Attempting to make our predicament into a game, Jane has us hold hands as we clomp down the stairs, directing us to pair up and scrounge the neighborhood garbage for some food. We've done it before, so we're not surprised at her directions.

I take Tom's hand and yell to the rest, "We're going to go behind the restaurant down the street." We find some chicken bones with some meat on them and a couple rolls. Tom pulls up his nose at the smell.

"You've got to eat it. It's all we have." I take a bite and form a weak smile. "See, it's fine." Tom follows my lead, as usual, and bites into the chicken.

Returning to our apartment, the others say they've found enough food to fill their bellies somewhat, too. Later, we all crawl into the same bed and Jane reads to us until the light extinguishes in the tiny apartment.

Because Tom is seventeen months younger than me, and often sick, I feel responsible for him. Tom snuggles in next to me. Soon he's snoring softly, but I can't sleep. I pray, "Please God, don't let them sell us, but if they do sell Tom, please let me go with him."

It's late when I hear our parents fumbling with the key to unlock the door outside the apartment. Jane gets up and lets them in. They stumble through the small space and flop onto their bed. Jane tiptoes back to her area on the bed, full of small bodies.

The chilly air wakes me the next morning. Mom and Dad lay on their bed in the same clothes they wore when they left yesterday. I'm not brave enough to get up without the others, so I scoot closer to my siblings and pretend to sleep.

After a while, a banging on the apartment door wakes us all. Mom plods across the bare
wood floor to answer it, her hair sticking out like brush bristles and her hose rolled down to her ankles.

I peek out from my spot on the bed. The guy at the door holds a tattered hat, and his worn suit pulls at the buttons around his middle. He barges in as soon as Mom opens the door.

Dad wakes and sits on the side of the bed. His gravelly voice sounds like a scratchy record. "Who are you?"

The man answers, staring at us in the other bed. "I'm here about the photo in the newspaper. I want to talk to you about making a deal."

I crawl out from under the covers and walk over and hug Mom, never wanting to let go. Tom follows and stands close to me. Mom begins to shake. Looking up, I expect tears, but her face contorts with anger. "George, don't you dare."

Dad grabs a sack and tosses Tom's few clothes into it. He nods my way. "Get your stuff."

I cling to Mom with more determination, but then Tom's face appears from behind her dress. I can't let him go alone. Maybe it'll only be for the summer, and we can come back for school in the fall. With tears clouding my vision, I add my clothes to the sack.

The man says, "Don't worry, ma'am, they'll be well cared for. We live on a farm; they'll love all the animals there." He moves toward us trying to add a smile to his stern face. "Come on, you two, we need to get going."

Dad yanks me away from Mom and gives my hand to the man. It feels sticky with sweat. I try to pull away, but his grip is firm. "No, I don't want to go."

Dad carries Tom and the sack of belongings and hurries out the door. The man follows, I flop on the floor and keep yelling. He picks me up like a sack of potatoes and traipses down the steps to the outside door, pushing it open with his foot. Both Dad and the guy take turns placing us in the back seat of his car. My throat feels like the bristles of a brush have rubbed it raw, and my screams become silent gasps.

Dad leans into the car and says, "Now, you both be good for Mr. VanVleet and his wife."

That's the last Tom and I see of our family.

Chapter 2

June 1951: Catherine

The long ride bouncing through the country in the old Chevy makes my head pound and my stomach queasy. Trying not to think about my own troubles, I try to comfort Tom, whose smaller hand clutches mine. He sits making loud whimpering noises beside me, and I can't help but think how much I wish I was the younger of us two, so I could let loose and cry, too.

Mr. VanVleet pulls off the road and turns to look at us. His dark beady eyes make me want to open the door and run. "Keep that kid quiet. I can't drive with all that racket back there."

I've never felt so scared, even when Dad would come home drunk and yell at all of us. On those occasions, I knew it was the drink that made him act mean. He always gave us big hugs the next day, and I loved him back.

Trying to convince myself as well, I whisper to Tom, "I think this is only for a visit. It won't be long, and Dad will come to get us." That seems to calm him a little and I feel better, too.

Tom falls asleep, and I watch as the city scape turns to a road edged with green grass and beyond, fields teeming with corn and beans. If only this was an outing with my family, the countryside would be a welcome change. I have never been far away from the city before, and I like what I see.

The old car smells like moist fabric, but a little fresh air whistles through the tiny cracks along the windows to give us some relief. A distinct change away from the urban odors drifts through the loose-fitting windows. My nose welcomes the new smells.

Chilly air makes me pull Tom even closer and my thoughts drift back to those times before we lived in the tenement. Tom's warm body reminds me of days not so long ago before Dad lost his job, when our whole family would sit in front of the warm fire in our former house where we all enjoyed being together as a family. Mom and Dad got along without fighting, and I can't remember ever being hungry then. Why couldn't it be that way again?

VanVleet says little as we continue our drive to the farm. Once out of the city traffic and driving is less worrisome, he glances back at me. I try not to meet his eyes. They fill me with dread. VanVleet's turned-down lips now emit a much gruffer voice, reminding me of my dad's after a night of drinking. "We don't have any kids, so you're going to make my wife so happy. It was her big idea to go get you two."

His grimace changes to a closed-lip smile when I focus on his reflection in the rear-view mirror. Shuddering, I turn away hoping he didn't see me staring.

When we arrive at the farm, Mr. VanVleet stops the car in front of a two-story house badly needing paint. He turns to the two of us huddled together in the back seat. Tom is now wide awake, his smaller body quivering against mine. "You will be expected to work. That's the main reason I agreed to bring you here. And you'll grow up in the fear of the Lord. The Bible says, spare not the rod, so make sure you do as you're told. Now get your things together and get out to meet your new mama."

While standing together at the side of the car, holding hands, tears trickle down Tom's cheeks, and I can feel him shaking. Wanting to be brave for his sake, I make up my mind to show no fear, so I bite the inside of my mouth to keep from crying. The metallic taste of blood fills the inside of my mouth making me feel sick.

A tall, lanky woman comes toward us from the dilapidated porch. She wears a faded house dress, clunky shoes, and an oversized sweater. Her severe bun is pulled back and fastened tightly behind her head, and the scowl on her face shows she wants no nonsense. She gives us each a slight welcome pat and says in a flat voice, "I will love you both. From now on, you will call me Mama." She motions for us to follow her into the house.

I look at Tom and see the confusion on his face. Feeling braver now, even though my insides churn from the bloody saliva and the ride in the rattly, old car, I yell, "No, our mama is back in the city. We want to go home."

The lady glares at me, grabs my arm and twists it. I nearly break down in tears, but my stubbornness kicks in.

"That's not going to happen. You need to obey me, or you'll get worse than this."

"Oww, that hurts." I rub my arm. A couple tears spill from my eyes and down my cheeks even though I try to hold them back.

Mr. VanVleet has parked the car closer to the barn and now walks up the path to the house. He stops in front of me and lifts my chin. "What's going on here? Don't be making Alice upset."

His stern face staring into mine makes my insides wiggle more. I can't hold it down. The heaving begins, and I empty my stomach on the drive almost on Mr.VanVleet's shoes.

"You'll clean that up later," says 'Mama.'

Alice gives both of us a shove toward the house door. Once inside, we follow her, not making any sounds, too scared to do anything else. She shows us where we'll sleep in the upstairs, unfinished bedrooms. No rugs cover the hardwood floors, but each small room holds an iron bed and one small dresser. One wool blanket lays at the foot of each bed, but no sheets cover the thin mattresses.

"Get settled," she says. "And then come down so we can get you started with your chores."

Trying to regain my courage, I give Tom a hug. "We'll be fine. Do what they say. Maybe this
will be a short visit. I'm sure Mom and Dad will come to get us before long, so we can start school in the city with the other kids. You'll be in first grade, and I'll be in second."

I want to believe this myself, but what if we end up going to school here in the country? I'll never see my family or my best friend, Cheryl, again. It all seems like a bad dream, but when I pinch my arm, pain is the only result.

Chapter 3

1951-1957: Catherine

After the first couple months with the VanVleets, it's obvious to both Tom and me, our new parents believe more in using the rod rather than spoiling the child. There are times when nothing we do pleases them, and the beatings come regardless of how we do our work. I long to see our parents and siblings in the city. My dreams are filled with former fun family times and sometimes I wake up sobbing to myself. I try to keep quiet, so Tom doesn't hear. Praying for Mom and Dad to come calms me some, and I fall back to sleep.

Using mostly traditional roles for boys and girls, the VanVleets assign Tom to help in the barn and garden, and my life centers around making meals, cleaning the house and doing laundry. The drudgery continues without stopping, day in and day out the same. I look forward to days when I can spend part of my hours at school. Schoolwork is easy for me, and I bask in the teachers' praise, so nonexistent in the VanVleets' home.

One of my chores is to wash the dishes after meals. I'm expected to dry each item before putting them back in the cupboards. But one evening, 'Mama' sees me putting the dishes away and drops of water still cling to some of the glasses. She slaps me on the back of my head, flinging it forward. Alice often uses this means as punishment because my thick brown hair covers any red mark.

"Oww, what'd I do?" Another slap comes. My anger burns inside my chest and my eyes shoot daggers toward her, but I don't say another word. I promise myself I won't let Alice make me cry ever again. She won't wear me down.

Another one of my jobs is gathering eggs from the chickens each morning. Sometimes the eggs are so fragile, they crack easily when I put them in the basket. On one occasion, I placed the basket in the sink, so the eggs can be washed and say, "Sorry, I laid them down as careful as I could, but a couple still cracked."

I'm surprised when Alice grabs the back of my neck and squeezes just enough that no marks result. I fight back the tears and calmly wash the eggs and put them into the refrigerator.

When Tom turns eleven and I'm twelve, Gerrit announces we're now old enough to begin helping with more of the farm chores. "After school, I'll need you to come out to the field to relieve me on the tractor, Tom, and I'll need Catherine to help with chores in the barn."

My eyes lock with Tom's. We focus on one another, and the fear that binds our lives together intensifies. I worry about Tom, driving the machinery while so young, but my job will be bad too. Being around Gerrit makes my skin crawl. I don't trust him. I have a suspicion about what he's thinking when he looks at me, and it's not fatherly love.

As the days continue, there's little Tom and I can do to please Gerrit. And Tom's troubles in the schoolyard make it worse for him at home. Sometimes the other boys taunt him with things like, "Holy jeans. Those tight shirts will be 'holy' too before long. The devil will be sure to leave you alone."

When Tom can't take it anymore, he lashes out, and one day he punches the closest kid. Mrs. DeKock, on the farm next to ours gets a phone call and comes to tell the VanVleets' to pick Tom up from school. He's sent directly to the barn to clean stalls. After dinner Gerrit rages, "You started that fight? What's wrong with you?" When Tom doesn't answer, Gerrit's face turns bright red. "Drop your pants and bend over, grab your ankles." Gerrit whips his belt from his waist and five red welts soon appear on Tom's white skin. "Go to the barn. You don't deserve a nice warm bed."

Alone in the cold upstairs for the first time since we arrived at the farm, I lay in my bed, shivering. I tiptoe to Tom's bed for his blanket, both to keep warm and to feel close to my dear brother. We've never been separated before, and it feels as if some part of me has been torn away. Imagining Tom alone in the barn makes sleep impossible.

When VanVleet goes to the barn to let Tom out the next morning, Tom climbs the stairs, and for a brief moment we can talk without someone listening. Tom describes the past night to me. "I fell asleep on the soft hay, but when VanVleet came to the barn, he made me move to a post rising from the cold cement and tied me to the post."

My fears become reality, but after that terrible night, calm settles in for a few weeks. Trying to mend our fences I suggest, "Tom, why don't you try to win Gerrit's approval by offering to mow the lawn with the push mower. Maybe he'll be less hard on you if you look for ways to help."

But Tom forgets to clean the underneath housing before putting the mower away and Gerrit uses a willow switch ten times across his backside. I watch the scene from my bedroom window, fists balled, wincing each time the switch crosses Tom's back and feeling increasing pain inside my belly. Why did I open my big mouth?

Later, when Tom comes in for the night, he sits on the bed next to me, head in his hands. I try to comfort him. "Oww, don't touch me."

I encourage him to remove his shirt and stealing down to the kitchen for a small bowl of cold water, I dab at his raw skin with the cool rag. I stammer, "I'm so sorry. It's all my fault."

"Don't ever say that. You're the only thing that makes this life bearable. If it wasn't for you, I'd blow this place."

No one around town has knowledge of how we're being treated. Not even the teachers at school or our Sunday School teachers realize how bad it is. When the punishment is severe enough to be visible, the VanVleets keep us home from school until the bruises are gone, or they make sure our clothing covers every inch of our skin. We're told to keep the beatings to ourselves, otherwise, we'll be punished more.

Discussing the days' events becomes our daily routine after school before going out to do our chores.

One day when I'm in eighth and Tom in seventh grade, we huddle together in my bedroom talking in hushed tones. My heart breaks when Tom stifles a sob as he shares his plight.

"I can't help it if I smell. The VanVleets make me go to school right after chores in the morning, so the other kids pinch their noses and move away when I come close."

Tears fill my eyes. "Maybe I can bring a towel and you can wash in the school bathroom."

"Naw, I figured out a way to make those kids pay. You should see them flinch when I throw eraser pieces or pencils at them when the teacher's back is turned. Other guys try it, but they can't hit a flea. Today one of the pencils I threw nicked the eye of the girl sitting next to me and she had to leave class. I suppose Gerrit and Alice will get another visit from Mrs. DeKock telling them they need to contact the school."

Tom's prediction is fulfilled and soon Gerrit yells for him to come down. All I hear is Gerrit's voice as he yells at Tom. Standing at the top of the stairs, I wrap my arms around my middle and with each loud crack from Gerrit's belt I grab a little tighter. Tom spends another night away from me in the barn and I toss and turn the whole night, praying over and over, "Please God, keep Tom safe."

Tom and I are expected to attend church services twice every Sunday since joining the VanVleets. During the services, I make sure I sit next to Alice, not next to Gerrit. I can't stand the thought of touching him. The years of grime and ineffectual washings give him the appearance of a mud-caked bush growing too close to the road.

After finishing our chores one Sunday, Tom and I are busy changing clothes when Alice yells, "Hurry and get cleaned up. We're going to be late. There's a meeting before church for the adults today."

With the bucket of cool water Tom has carried upstairs, we wash as well as possible. Changing into our Sunday clothes, I notice the barn smell still lingers in Tom's hair, but I don't have time to help him wash it out. Will the other boys make comments even at church?

The service moves forward with the usual doctrinal sermon and strict ritualistic format. No one smiles much, and everyone sits and prays or meditates before the service starts while the organist plays softly in the background. The sermon, filled with God's wrath on sinners, again puzzles me.

"God is love, and all who live in love, live in God, and God lives in them. God is love, and he who abides in love abides in God, and God in him." quotes my young Sunday School teacher when we leave the service for our individual classes. All I can think is, how can a loving God let people like Gerrit and Alice have kids?

At Sunday lunch, Alice asks, "What did you learn today at church?"

I don't answer but continue to look down at my food and move it from one side of my plate to the other. I find none of God's love in the VanVleet's house.

Tom says the same thing he always says after church. "If we're bad, we won't go to heaven."

"So, where do you think you're going?" asks Gerrit with that nasty smirk he saves mainly for Tom.

Tom stares back at him. "Hell, I guess."

"You better change your ways, then boy."

Gerrit scares me. Taking a small bite, my thoughts drift to how I can stay safe during my afternoon chores. He watches me constantly, waiting for his chance to get close. Most days I can hide by helping Alice inside the house, but sometimes Gerrit and I work together in the barn and Tom is elsewhere. My plan is to do my chores as quickly as possible and when finished, excuse myself to work on my homework. My high grades may be my ticket out of here someday.

Chapter 4

March 1961: Tom

The fun begins at night. I wait in the drafty barn, unable to move from my prison. My sixteen-year-old body is pulled tight against the barn's post. The length of rope that tethers me also secures my hands and fingers. My joints tingle with numbness. The longer I sit, the more hate fills my chest.

Scurrying noises on the cold concrete floor keeps me alert. The rodents get braver as the dark settles in, but there's nowhere I can go. I'm afraid to sleep. I sit and rest against the pole, watching for their beady eyes in the dark, using my boots as weapons. The first rat ventures close, but I kick it away. It skitters off into the darkness again. Imagining a rat chewing on my skin makes my insides quiver. Visions of large rodents flash before me. My head nods to my chest but I bounce back awake, jerking up with a hard bump against the splintered wood of the pole.

For three days, I've been enduring my punishment tied to this post by my so-called father. Keeping vigilant is my challenge. Short naps a few times during the daylight hours when the sun streams through the cracks between the old siding become my only rest. That small amount of light is enough to keep the varmints hidden. I'm not sure if these small animals can harm me, but I don't want to find out. So, I wait again as the darkness creeps into the space like a panther stealing through the brush. My stomach gurgles with its emptiness. The floor grows cold and damp below my bottom and shivering begins. I'm so cold. I clutch my arms as close to my body as possible with tied hands to control the shaking. Concentrating on what I will do someday when I can leave this place helps to pass the time. I begin to plan what I can do if Gerrit returns.

At least, tonight, the moonlight filtering through the barn's siding gives some respite from the darkness. There's more scurrying even in the dim light. The rats move out from their hiding places, hoping to find a few morsels. I check my small area, ensuring no crumbs are left from my one meal today, a glass of milk and a peanut butter sandwich.

When Gerrit brought the lunch, he kicked me a couple times and slapped my head to make his point. "Apologize and I'll let you come back into the house."

My silent stare makes him turn and leave again. I will never give him the title of father with the way he treats us. No hugs and kind words ever come from that man. I hate him more every day.

Adjusting my legs as much as possible, I try not to think of the pressure building up in my groin. My thoughts turn to Catherine. Who knows what Gerrit will do if Catherine is alone with him? I can't stand the way the old man has been looking at her the last couple of months. Is he expecting sex as part of her household duties? My breathing deepens just thinking about the possibility. I shake my head to get those thoughts to disappear.

Another rat comes close, waking me from my reverie, and I kick it away. I sit on guard listening to the night sounds, the wind whistling through the barn siding, wings fluttering as birds move from one rafter to another. The cows' soft breathing lulls me to relax. I slump forward, close to sleep, my tethered hands falling between my legs.

Small pinpricks at first. I flip my arms up and down, hitting my tied wrists too hard on the concrete. Pain shoots up my arm. A rogue rodent skitters off into the darkness. Others react and run to hide. Staying awake becomes my goal and now my full bladder helps to keep me from nodding off. The other times Gerrit came with food, he let me relieve myself, but not today. Will I have to empty my bladder while sitting here? I can't let that happen.

Planning my escape fills my thoughts. Maybe old Gerrit will come tonight to let me loose. If he does, I'll be ready for him. My mind is made up. This will be the last time Gerrit will punish me by tying me like a slave. I'm sixteen, old enough to be on my own, but I've got to convince Catherine to come with me. She always resists when I try to talk to her about leaving, saying it's different for a girl to run away. I've got to convince her.

I focus on Lady, the cow in the nearby stall to clear my head. Lady's large liquid eyes look as if she might be commiserating with my plight. Tired of standing, she has chosen to lie down in the hay. What I wouldn't give for some of that soft hay under my cold bottom. The farm animals have made my stay here bearable. I talk to them without worrying that my words will be misunderstood. Sometimes I've taken my anger out on the chickens by throwing rocks at them, thinking they're doomed for the pot anyway, but afterwards, I feel bad and give them extra feed.

Alice always assigns the butchering task to us. Catherine cries each time we need to take care of the nasty business, but I've learned to harden myself to the job. Without butchering, there will be no fried chicken dinner, and I love fried chicken. Catherine often refuses to eat it after dealing with all the blood, but old Gerrit stuffs it into her mouth until she gags and eventually swallows. He's the devil in farmer's garb when he treats Catherine that way. I long to punish him the same way he does us. Tonight, I will punish him.

My heart pounds with rage, and those thoughts hang like icicles inside my head, freezing in time. Trying to calm myself, I focus on my plan of action for when Gerrit arrives. Waiting is like not being able to avoid an oncoming tornado. If he doesn't come soon, urine will spill onto the floor and the rats will take over skittering through it.

The sound of heavy footsteps tramping outside the barn door alerts me. The old door creaks as Gerrit pushes it open, his galoshes unbuckled, making each step a loud clomp. He walks toward me with head bowed, and arms clasped behind his back and stops. The silence is as soft as snow falling on the roof, making my shoulders feel as if they will crack below the weight of it.

The stillness breaks with Gerrit's horrible voice. "Look at me."

I raise my head, stare into those awful eyes, so full of hatred, below the bill of his dingy cap. He's not a tall man, but strong from years of work. The same overalls he's worn for days on end cover his body, only being changed if overly greasy from chores. A Carhart jacket wraps his upper body. Maybe Gerrit's extra layers will make him less agile, an easier target.

"Ready to apologize to your mama for saying the roast was dry?" Gerrit asks, his voice low and gruff as usual.

I nod but don't reply. Gerrit pulls out his pocketknife and holds it high taunting me with a slow release. "I said, are you sorry for what you said, boy?"

I grunt, "Sorry."

Gerrit bends and begins cutting the rope from my hands. Blood rushes the feeling back into them as he works to free my feet. The rope bursts apart with a jerk, and the knife flips from Gerrit's hand for a moment. I see my chance and grab for the handle just as Gerrit lunges also. We both grapple for the upper hand, but my strength becomes too much for the older man. I bash Gerrit's knife hand against the rough-hewn post repeatedly, jubilant within, feeling the power flood through my body. Blood splatters onto the floor and the knife flips into the air and lands on the cement with a loud clank. Lady raises her large head to view the scene and moans in empathy. I hustle to grab the knife and jab as Gerrit charges forward. The steel edge enters below his rib cage. My joy turns to panic.

Gerrit's eyes expand to saucers, and his grotesque face falls along with his crumpled body. As Gerrit falls to the floor, blood pools below him. He groans as his breathing quiets.

Dread creeps up from the bottom of my toes and works its way into my memory. I store the
scene away, hoping never to see that much blood again. I rush, panic stricken, from the barn
and into the house, past the living room where Alice dozes, and up the stairs to Catherine's room.

"I stabbed him!" I gasp, stopping inside the barren room. "I've got to get away."

Catherine wakes and turns on the lamp next to her bed. "What? Who?" A light dawns in her eyes. Sitting up and gathering the blanket around her shoulders, she rubs the sleep from her eyes.

Trembling in anticipation, I wait for her to wake fully. Catherine shivers from the cold inside the unheated bedroom. Bare wooden floors and drafty windows make the room cold even in March.

"What should I do, Catherine? I don't want to go without you, but…"

"I was afraid something like this would happen someday." Catherine stands to put her arms around me. "You've got to go. Don't worry about me. I'll be okay if I stay close to Alice."

"Tom, what are you doing in here?" I turn to see Alice standing in the doorway, her wild eyes and unkept hair making her look menacing.

I run from the room, pushing Alice roughly aside. With each step downward, I hear my own breath getting louder through my nostrils.

Chapter 5

March 1961: Tom

Alice calls out in pain from the shove I've given her. But from the placement of her voice, I can tell she hasn't fallen down the stairs. Thank goodness, I haven't caused another death. So, I do the only thing I can right now, ignoring the two at the top of the stairs, I hurry the rest of the way down toward the kitchen. My head aches as I stop and look up from the bottom of the stairs. How can I leave the one person who has loved me unconditionally?

Catherine, framed by the light shining from her room, helps Alice get up to stand beside her. Each yells something different.

"Run as far and fast as you can," Catherine shouts.

"Come back here, Tom. Don't you dare leave this farm," Alice snarls. "You won't get far. The police'll be out looking for you."

Standing still for a moment, I'm unable to decide and lift my hands to Catherine as if questioning. Contorting my face into a sad jack-o-lantern, I try to communicate to Catherine how hard it is to leave her. She points toward the door and mouths the word, 'Go,' and makes an imperceptible goodbye wave. Her eyes glisten from the hall light, full of tears, but after a bit, her lips part in a smile. My heart begins to settle down to its regular rhythm.

Moving into the kitchen, I grab some of the bread Alice baked today from the kitchen table and a warm jacket from the hook by the door. A small flashlight on the shelf catches my eye, and I take that too. So what if I'm accused of being a thief. It's nothing compared to what I've already done in the barn. I'll never be able to get the picture of Gerrit's face out of my mind as the knife slid into his chest.

Outside, the moonlight no longer fills the sky, and the wind picks up. A small amount of light filters through the clouds and a few drops begin to fall while I head away from the house. Instead of the busy county road that borders the VanVleet farm on the west, I take the familiar path behind the barn that leads to the field road, worn flat by tractor tires. I can follow this track until I come out on another county road one mile to the east. The rain starts falling harder, so this warm jacket is a godsend. The biting raindrops sting my face and I shield my eyes by holding my arm to my forehead. Plodding forward, away from that hell, I can't help but feel more content as I hurry along.

After about ten minutes of walking in the wind and rain, not making much headway, I see headlights near the one-lane bridge on the south side of town. But there's something not right about the direction they shine. The beams glow too high, like one of those spotlights businesses hire for a sale. Picking my way closer to the light, I scan the area for movement. I don't want to be caught before getting out of Stockwell, so I hesitate to spend any extra time checking this out.

But as I move closer, something seems terribly wrong with the scene. The car's lights aren't in line with the bridge. Straining to see through the rain is like looking through misted glass. I move faster while trying to sort out in my mind what I should do. If someone needs help, I'll have to somehow contact the police. I don't want to go back to the hell I just left, but I wouldn't feel right about passing by someone who needs help, either.

Moving ahead, I see why the car's headlights shine into the night sky at such an odd angle. Even in the darkness, I can now make out the shape of a vehicle far to the right of the bridge, rear end down, standing on end in a small feeder ditch draining into the larger ditch the county road crosses. My feet stumble over torn-up sod and muddy tracks showing the path the car must have followed as it probably flipped over several times before its final demise.

I call several times, trying to make myself heard above the rain and wind. "Anyone there?"

Lightning brightens the sky, and I spot a body sprawled several feet from the car. My legs feel like rubber as I run to the spot and call, "You okay?"

But the lifeless form remains still. I stoop and turn the person over with care, gagging at the sight and feeling as if I might lose the small amount in my stomach. The face is so bruised and cut that it's beyond recognition. I bend to listen for breath and feel the guy's neck for a pulse, but there's nothing. I've forgotten about the flashlight that falls from my jacket pocket when I stand. Bending again to pick it up, I flip on the beam, and scan the area, trying to see if anyone else has met the same fate. I want to hurry away from this mess, but I can't ignore the feeling deep down in my gut telling me to stay and try to help.

I call several times, "Anyone here?" Stopping after each call, I listen for a moan, a faint sigh, a cough, possibly? Only the wind answers. Walking forward again, I scan the accident perimeter for signs of life. I need to move on, but I can't until I know if I'm able to help. It wouldn't be right to leave before I've checked the whole area. I want to do the right thing. Down deep, I've always wanted to be a good person. Maybe helping will make up for what I've done to Gerrit.

I inch toward the ditch on the chance that someone might still be caught in the car. Leaning against one bank, it stands like a misplaced giant surfboard. I slide down the grass to see if any remnants of life may be inside. Shining my dim flashlight across the front seat reveals an empty crater, seats without passengers, and a shattered missing windshield. Relief spreads over me for a moment.

But as I climb back up the wet grass to the bank's top, a low moaning reaches my ears from the other side of the ditch. Down again, holding onto the car's frame, I manage to cross the water, soaking my clothes even more than the incessant rain has.

The faint light of the flashlight, almost dead now, outlines the origin of the moans. Rushing to the side of the sound's source, I find another unrecognizable person. His right leg is mangled, his left severed at the knee, and his arms are bent in non-human poses. Breaths come in erratic gasps, if at all. I have all I can do again to keep from losing the contents of my stomach. I know enough not to try to move the body, so I lower my mouth as close as possible. "I'll get help. Hang on a little while longer."

"No," the boy manages to croak. "Stay with me. I'm scared. Please."

Wrestling with myself, pretty sure this life has little chance of surviving, I also wonder if I can save him by getting help. Lightning hits again, and I get a better picture of the situation. The boy's eyes are wide with terror, and in that moment, I recognize him. He's a year ahead of me in school. It's Jed Thomas, the star basketball player. I've often envied his athletic ability, good grades and parents who love him, but here he is pleading for me, a nobody, to stay with him. My insides turn to mush and tears add to the raindrops on my face. I search my brain for a way to help.

Sitting down next to Jed, I begin doing the only thing the monster I lived with has taught me. I pray to a God I'm not sure exists, but I don't know what else to do. Praying aloud, I try to mimic the pastor's prayers, and it seems to calm Jed. I've never had to pray in a life and death situation but praying comforts me also. Maybe there is something to this God thing.

Moments pass after I finish my prayer, the only sounds, the rain hitting the car's metal and an occasional thunderclap. Jed's breathing becomes softer and more ragged, then stops entirely. I wait a moment more, calling Jed's name repeatedly, but there's no response. With nothing more I can do, sobbing, and with shaking hands, I close Jed's eyes.

Panic fills my thoughts, but I try to pull myself together. I need to move on. Someone else will come along and call the police before long. An idea stumbles through the connections in my brain, wobbling back and forth through my nerve networks until I justify it to myself.

Touching another dead person creeps me out, but Jed has died only seconds ago, so it's not like it will be that hard. Pulling aside Jed's honor jacket, I fumble for a wallet. Nothing there. I hesitate, then with trembling hands, I flip what's left of Jed to his side, checking his jeans' pockets, and I have success. Jed's wallet balances in my cold fingers.

With shaking hands, inside the wallet, I find everything I need to become a new person, Jed's driver's license, and enough cash to get me far enough down the road to hitch a ride west.

Chapter 6

March 1961: Catherine

After Tom departs the night of the fight, Alice and I dash through the rain to find Gerrit sprawled on the cold concrete of the barn floor. The blood flows from his body like little rivers with nowhere to go. Alice falls to his side and lifts his head into her lap. Her screams fill the night air inside the barn and echo from the rafters. The sound of those screams wakens something in Gerrit, and his eyes flick open.

"Thank you, Lord, he's alive!" Alice yells. "Catherine, run to the neighbor's house and call the police."

I back away from the scene, clutching my stomach, sure now why Tom needed to leave. Offering a silent prayer that Tom has found a ride away from this awful place, I run the whole way to the neighbor's house ignoring the rain and wind. My breath comes in huge gulps while banging on their door. Raindrops fall from my soaked hair and my housecoat hangs limp and wet around my shoulders.

Mrs. DeKock comes to the door, wiping sleep out of her eyes and clutching her robe around her. "Catherine, what in the world? What's the matter?"

My words spill out like a whirlwind. "Mama sent me to use the phone. May I? It's her husband, Gerrit. He needs a doctor terribly, but I'm supposed to call the police."

"Sure, come in. I'll dial it for you."

When the police answer, I stutter out the news, "You've got to come to the VanVleet farm. I think Gerrit might be almost dead. There's lots of blood." I feel myself start to faint and flop down on the chair near the phone.

Mrs. DeKock grabs the receiver from me and gives the officers the address. She lifts my chin up and looks into my face with eyes full of sympathy. "They'll be there as soon as they can pull some officers away from a bad accident south of town. A couple teenagers are dead after leaving tonight's basketball game." She delivers this message with a pat to my shoulder and offers to drive me back to the farm, but I refuse.

"I'll be fine. Thanks anyway."

I sit for a few minutes dripping more water onto the rug near the phone table, and then hurry out the door before Mrs. DeKock can insist again on driving me. No one else needs to see what happened. The gossip will be bad enough for Tom the way it is. Keeping the story contained might save him from some of the scandal.

Running through the black night, the storm intensifies, and I slow to a snail's pace. While plodding ahead, I try to erase the scene between Tom and Gerrit from my imagination and clear my head for what lies ahead.

When I return to the VanVleets, Alice has found an old blanket and uses part of it for a makeshift pillow and the rest for a covering for Gerrit's shivering body. She sits by his side on the barn floor, holding his hand. Her eyes show no tears. In the dim light of the barn, Alice's skin, drained of all color, stands out in contrast to the bright blood stain on the middle of her housecoat. I shudder with revulsion and cold. I've never seen this much blood, not even after butchering a hen for Sunday dinner. Even that amount of blood makes me sick, and this is tons more in comparison.

"Well, are they coming?" Alice has recovered her composure and her sharp tongue.

I stay as far from the bloody scene as I can. Void of any feelings for the adults sitting on the barn floor, my insides spin like a tornado, swirling with indecision, fear, anger and frustration. If I wish for Gerrit to die, Tom will be in more trouble, but his dying will solve many of my own problems.

Doubling over and grabbing at my queasy belly, I answer without thinking about what I'm saying. "The officer said they're short-handed. There's been a bad accident south of town. A couple of teenagers are dead in a wreck after the basketball game. The one you wouldn't let me go to. They'll send someone as soon as they can."

"You're worried about not going to a game? Your father has been stabbed, and that's all you can think about? I should whip you, but they'll be walking in here any minute. All we need is for the police to get nosey. They'll be asking too many questions anyway about why your brother stabbed him. You let me do the talking when they get here, understand?"

I nod my head but don't answer, fear replacing my other emotions. Instead, I move further back and lean against Lady's stall as if the cow can protect me. Lady nuzzles my hand where I hold onto the worn rough boards, reminding me life is still worth clinging to. The cold night air penetrates my wet pajamas and robe, and I pull the fabric tighter to my midsection to keep from trembling.

"I said, do you understand?"

I nod my head and look down at the floor. "Yes, I don't want to talk to them, anyway."

Time ticks by like slowly opening flower petals. Gerrit moans every few minutes, and more blood flows, extending the little streams. If Gerrit dies, Tom will be accused of murder, but if he lives, my life will remain a living hell. My mind again churns with what I should hope for. Guilt enters into my conflict. I need to set aside what's good for me and think of Tom. Wanting Gerrit to live becomes my prayer.

After another half hour, help comes. The police apologize for their delay, saying the incident involving the teens took most of their force this evening. Gerrit is rushed to the hospital and admitted. After several intense hours, he's stabilized and told he'll need to stay in the hospital for several days.

Chapter 7

March 1961: Tom

I make my way from the accident, trying to put the sight of the dead boys out of my mind. I can't help either now. I justify taking the money and license since Jed can't use it ever again. Someone else will come along soon and report the wreck, and the accident may keep the small-town police force busy. Alice will be calling the police soon, too, but they'll be slow to make it to the farm and give me the time I need to get far from Stockwell. I should be feeling remorse for hurting Gerrit, but my only concern is for Catherine.

The rain subsides and walking down the county road toward the main highway becomes easier. Once I reach the main thoroughfare, I'll be able to catch a ride west and, before long, find work there. The busy state highway may increase my chances of being spotted, but there's also a much better chance of hitching a ride. My plan becomes staying off in the grass far from the edge of the road until I can spot a semi going west.

Headlights coming at a high-speed move toward me

from not too far away. I pick up my pace. My wet boots and jeans become heavier with each step. Shivering from the chill of my damp clothes next to my skin and the wet cloth irritating the edges of my arms, I stop to lift my crumpled socks up out of my boots. As bad as I feel right now, not even these conditions can make me want to return.

The intersection of the county road and the highway looms ahead. Reaching it, I run across to the side of the road leading west, slowing and trudging through the grass berm. The long, wet grass and dirt squish under my boots, and my trek slows to the speed of a turtle.

Thoughts circle through my head as I trudge along. Trying to block out the pictures in my mind of the two dead teens a little older than myself, I try instead to think about what lies ahead. I know all about farming. At least that's something good that came from staying with the VanVleets. Maybe I'll be able to work at one of the big farms in Kansas or Nebraska. I heard some of the men at church discussing how their relatives manage huge farms out there. I can handle the work if it doesn't involve the kind of treatment old Gerrit inflicts. How can a man act so religious in front of the other people at church and be so awful to Catherine and me when we're at home? My fists become as tight as a knotted rope when I think about his eyes as the knife plunged into his chest, but I'm not sorry. The way he treated us was not right.

The low rumble of traffic stirs me out of my reverie, and I force myself to calm down. I turn to see disks of light heading toward me from a short distance away. As the truck comes closer, the noisy engine indicates a big semi rig, just the ticket I need out of this town.

Lumbering up the bank to the edge of the highway, I extend my arm and thumb. Will a driver be able to notice something so small in the dark, much like a bobber in a vast lake? I smile to myself at the image. If only I was. I could float away and never come back.

The truck blows past, spraying me with a muddy mist. Discouragement penetrates, a sinking feeling tying my gut into knots. Maybe I'll never attract a ride. My soaked clothes irritate my skin with every move, making my steps drudgery. Again, walking far from the pavement to keep from being seen unless by choice, makes moving difficult through the uncut taller grass, keeping my progress slow. The cold works its way deeper into my core. I yell "Why? What did I do to deserve this?"

If only our parents hadn't given us to the VanVleets. Thoughts slam from one side of my brain to the other with each step. A hopeful thought surfaces. Maybe Mom and Dad are doing better now, and they'll come to get Catherine. My spirits lift just thinking about this possibility.

Again, traffic sounds begin behind me. Two cars pass, but I don't try for those in case it's someone from Stockwell who might know me. Another semi approaches, making the distinct sound of downshifting. It slows, and I hurry to the road and wave like a mad man. The ground rumbles beneath my feet as the driver applies the brake.

When the truck rolls to a stop, the driver reaches over to turn down the passenger window. "Saw you in the car headlights as they passed. What gives?"

I tip my cap back and look up at the driver, hoping being straightforward will gain the guy's trust. "Could you give me a ride? I need to get to my aunt and uncle's farm in Nebraska to help them with chores. My uncle's taken sick."

"Kind of late to be traveling, don't you think?"

I keep my gaze on the driver. "Yeah, but my mom got word this afternoon. She's worried, so she said I better get going right away."

The truck driver stares at me for what seems like ages, probably trying to decide if he wants to take a chance on me. "All right, get in, but I'm not going that far."

I thank the guy and climb in. As we travel, the warm air blowing toward my feet begins drying my wet clothes, and a distinctive odor fills the semi-cab. The driver doesn't complain or say much at all, but the endless chatter of the radio talk show fills the night air with constant sound. Soon my chin drops to my shirt, and sleep tiptoes over my frame.

Waking when the truck comes to a jerky stop, I stretch and rub the sleep from my eyes. Inside the cab, the warm air causes moisture to cling to the window. I straighten and wipe it dry with my elbow so I can see through the glass.

"Hey, sorry I woke you. This old thing rattles and thumps whenever I need to make a quick stop. Going through this city will keep you awake."

"Where are we?" I ask, wide awake now.

"Princeton, halfway across Illinois." The driver gives the rig the gas, and the truck bumps along as he changes gears with so much clatter to get up to speed that it's impossible to talk. I look out the window as a typical scene of city businesses passes by.

Once the truck's noise subsides a little, I turn back

to the driver. "Guess I've been sleeping quite a while."

"Snoring, too. Never heard such snorts." The guy laughs and gives a couple of snorts himself.

I settle back and try to stay awake. I don't want to say anything in my sleep that might give away my actual reason for traveling. The police will be looking for me soon, but I can't let the driver know that.

The truck rumbles on, and before long, my thoughts turn back to Catherine, hoping she will be okay. I can't put away the feeling of guilt I have for leaving her with the VanVleets. She's the only family I have now. What if something happens and I never get to see her again. Tears form in the corners of my eyes, and I wipe them quickly away.

The truck driver's words clip through my thoughts and cut into the fog of my disturbing memories. My survival impulses kick in when I hear him say, "I can't take you any farther. This is where I need to deliver my load." The guy pulls the truck into a big distribution warehouse parking area and begins backing it up to the loading dock.

I gather my few belongings. At least my clothes and boots have dried enough to make moving more comfortable. When the driver stops to check his bearings, I climb down from the massive vehicle and yell, "Thanks for the lift, mister. Hope I can give someone else a favor to repay yours someday."

"Good luck, kid." He gives me a thumbs up with a smile as broad as the semi-cab.

Chapter 8

March 1961: Tom

As I stand on the pavement near the enormous truck, I wave while the driver backs farther into the unloading dock area. Moving out of the way of the semi and watching the driver's backing skill for a few minutes makes me wonder whether I'll ever be able to handle a rig with the talent this truck driver friend demonstrates. After watching for a few more seconds, I turn to leave, looking from left to right, not sure where I'll be led next.

The eastern sky's warm glow begins to peek above the horizon as I saunter toward the street that leads away from the trucking company. The streetlamp also glows, adding artificial light to the slender morning rays mirroring my feeling of hope for a new day.

I smile to myself. Is this what freedom feels like? But then a cloud enters my thoughts. I'll never be able to be truly happy as long as I know Catherine is still with old Gerrit. I have to keep going and make a way for both of us. This pain in my chest initiates a promise to struggle onward, putting aside doubts that we'll ever be reunited.

Moving along the awakening street, I follow the sidewalk until more businesses line either side of the road. Restaurants, several clothing stores, a hardware store, and a second-hand store all indicate a busy thoroughfare. My stomach clenches and emits a loud rumble. I haven't eaten much in the past three days; only the little Gerrit had tossed my way while tied up in the barn and the bread I'd taken when running from the house.

A small café catches my eye on the other side of the street. After crossing over the silent morning pavement, the closed sign on the front window looms larger. Seeing the sign makes the hollow space inside my belly grow to an immense balloon. I park myself on the bench outside the door, legs stretched out, arms folded around my body for warmth, and wait for the restaurant to open. There's no big hurry to move west now. I'm far enough away from Stockwell to be safe from being recognized.

Hearing myself snore softly, I jump a little when I catch the click of the doorknob lock and turn to see the waitress flip the closed sign to open. Two guys dressed in gray uniforms as if for work, pull open the door to go in, and the little bell above the door sounds a welcome. I check the wallet to make sure the money is still there, open the door, and take a wooden stool at the green laminated L-shaped counter diagonal from the two workers.

Besides the counter stools, the little diner holds several four-person tables lined along the outside walls, empty so far. Red and white checked curtains hang only for decoration on the three windows, and dark-beige stained carpet covers the floor. The aroma of coffee and bacon cooking fills the air, and my stomach grumbles a calling.

"What can I get you?" asks the red-headed young waitress, snapping her gum as she talks. I wait to see if the guys who entered before me will answer, but they sit in silent repose, studying the menu.

The less money I use, the better chance I can get more miles away from VanVleet's farm and further west. I can't spend much, so I don't need a menu. "I'll have two eggs and an order of toast and coffee."

I start reading the free newspaper lying on the counter, scanning the headlines for news of a murder back in Indiana, but it turns out to be only a local paper. After the waitress takes the two guys' orders, surprised by a loud question from the other side of the bar, I jerk my head up.

"Where you headed?" The dark-haired guy with an acne-pocked face repeats the question when I don't answer. "I said, where you headed?"

I glance behind myself, unsure who the guy's talking to, but we're the only three in the restaurant this early. So, I answer with the same story I told the truck driver. The next time someone questions me, I can easily remember what I tell different people if I keep my story the same, and maybe strangers will be less suspicious. "I'm hitch-hiking to Nebraska. My aunt and uncle need me to help on their farm."

"Yeah? Maybe we'll skip swork and head west, too," the smaller blond guy says, giving his friend a tap on the arm. His stare lasts until my food arrives, making my insides jittery. I keep busy, preparing my food, grabbing the salt and pepper from the display, and taking my time spreading jelly on my toast. When I look back at the two guys, they continue to watch as I take my first bite. So, what is with these guys?

Their huge breakfasts arrive, and they finally occupy themselves eating and drinking with loud slurping and smacking after each mouthful. I try to make my meager breakfast last by chewing slowly, but the delicious smell of ham and bacon from their plates makes me wish for more.

I had hoped to spend as much time as possible in the warm restaurant, but these guys aren't giving me a good feeling about hanging out here. After my initial impression of them as workers, I notice their shabby clothing, dirty hands, and unruly hair under their caps. If they are heading to work, their workplace must not care about appearances.

"How much do I owe?" I call, wanting to get away from their stares. Grabbing the unfamiliar wallet in my jeans' pocket, it slips to the floor displaying the stack of bills. After I gather the wallet from the grubby carpet, I catch the blond standing up from his stool, looking over the counter and checking out the scene.

The blond guy moves around the bar and closer to me. "Hey, what's your hurry? We can show you to the tracks south of town. Heard there's a train coming through about eight that could take us a long way west. Wait a bit, and we can all head together."

I catch the waitress's eye. She shrugs and turns, not helping me with my decision like she doesn't want to get involved. So, I pay my bill and wait, my fingers idly drumming the counter. I don't have many other options, having little idea where Princeton is or how to proceed out of this city.

As they talk, I discover the blond man's name is Dave. He's the one who does most of the talking. "This here is Bubba." Dave slaps the dark-haired guy on the shoulder.

The name Bubba fits his appearance. His frame flows over the small stool, and when Bubba straightens, still sitting, he's a good six inches taller than Dave. Both guys act decent, so maybe I can trust them after all. My full stomach calms and strength returns to my body.

Dave points his thumb toward the Men's Restroom sign, indicating we should each use the facilities before leaving. When we leave the café, the sun's rays begin to warm the air, and my mood brightens, too. I walk one step behind the duo, humming a little made-up tune. Soon I'll be in Nebraska and be able to look for a job as a farm hand.

I point to a clock in the jewelry store window showing seven-fifteen. "Look at the time."

"We better hurry. Don't want to miss the train," Dave says, and laughter fills the morning air as if we three are old friends.

Walking several more blocks toward the south and over two sets of railroad tracks, we arrive at the freight yard. Dave leads us to a long freight train idling on the far set of the tracks. A railroad worker walks along, checking each freight car to make sure the doors are closed and locked. We dodge out of sight behind a pile of freight boxes. My forehead beads up with sweat.

Dave whispers, "Follow me."

We climb over the coupling between two rail cars to the opposite side and pick the first open car. Grabbing a c-shaped bar attached to the floor of the car, Dave uses it as a handle, pulls himself up and crawls into the empty freight car. I go next with Bubba giving me an extra push. Dave and I each grab one of Bubba's arms and help him up into the dark space.

"How often have you guys done this?" I ask as I try to accustom my eyes to the dark space.

"Plenty of times, right Bubba?"

Bubba wobbles his head up and down and says, "Yep."

Dave starts for the darkest corner. "The railroad guy'll be coming along, so let's each grab a corner. Once the door is closed, we can move back out."

I do as I'm told, heading to a corner. When I slump down onto the dirty boxcar floor, it reminds me of the cold barn floor. Small slits of light filter through the wood joints, and my eyes begin to adjust so I can distinguish the contents of the nearly empty freight car. Only a few large wooden boxes are stacked in the middle close to the door.

After a few minutes, flashlight beams sweep around the cavernous inside but don't hit the corners where the three of us are hiding. The groaning of the door sliding shut makes me shudder, visualizing what a jail stay may be like. I wait for some sign from the others before I move from my spot. The train begins to pull out from the station, bumping and jerking along as it starts down the tracks. I curl into myself, afraid of what the future holds.

Dave makes it across the car without me noticing and stands before me, scaring me out of my skin. "We can move around anywhere in here now, but we may as well get comfortable. It's going to be all day before we stop again."

We settle near the storage boxes where there's brighter light, and each grabs a spot to lounge. The train picks up speed, and the train's wheels clacking away become mesmerizing. Soon all three of us are dozing.

When we wake up a couple hours later, Bubba offers us some leftover bacon from breakfast, not much but still a welcome surprise. My fears subside somewhat. Maybe these two are legit.

I stand to stretch. "Do you think we're coming close to the next stop? It's getting dark outside."

"No way of tellin'. Just have to sit tight." Dave stands and moves in close to me, legs wide and chest puffed out. "Where'd you get all that cash you're carrying? Steal it?"

I don't answer. I slide my hand over my back pocket, protecting the billfold. Out of the corner of my eye, I notice Bubba getting up too.

"How about you let us count it for you?"

I back away, but with a nod from Dave, Bubba grabs me from behind, and Dave takes the wallet from my pocket.

"Give that back." I struggle, but it's no use against those beefy arms.

"Oh, I'll give it back, all right." Dave takes the money from the wallet, shoves it in his pocket, and crams the billfold back into my pants. He loosens my belt and whips it from the belt loops in one quick pull. While Bubba holds tight, Dave wraps the belt around my torso, pinning my arms to my body and tightening the belt. He grabs a dirty hankie from his own pocket and ties it around my mouth and behind my head. My mumbled protests are lost inside the fabric.

"Give me your belt," he says to Bubba, but Bubba only stares at Dave. "All right, I'll use mine." He takes it off, shoves me up against a freight box, and binds my feet with the belt.

Bubba releases me and drops me to a sitting position, leaning me against one of the other boxes. I try to make some pleading sounds, but the two ignore me. Flitting my eyes back and forth like the speed of a train is the only thing I can do to try to stay safe.

Another couple hours pass before the train's movement starts to slow. Bubba and Dave carry me to a dark corner, and they each hide again in one of the other corners. Finally, time moves forward, and the door opens. Some type of machine revs up nearby. The tines of a forklift move into the car to unload the boxes. More waiting. Dave and Bubba amble to the open door and peek around it.

"Adios, Amigo," Dave says as he and Bubba climb down from the railcar.

I scoot my bottom along the dirty floor until I reach the open door and flip my feet outside the car. When I hear the sound of a man's voice I exhale a huge breath, smiling behind the rag.

"Looks like they hood-winked you."

My eyes land on the man who's staring at me. He wears a tan uniform with a bright, shiny star pinned to his chest. His round belly comically strains the buttons on his tight-fitting shirt, but the belt and gun holster show he's the real thing. All my fears tumble into my stomach. My plans of traveling farther west crash to the ground along with the sheriff's assistance down from the railcar.

Chapter 9

April 1961: Tom

After the Sheriff takes me from the train and unties the gag, I am loaded in the back seat of the squad car and taken to the station. When we arrive at the station, I describe the other two riders the best I can. My voice cracks and tears are close to the surface, but I manage to hold them in. I say nothing about the stolen money in my statement because, technically, it wasn't my money. It's probably gone for good, anyway.

"Sorry, kid. We'll have to hold you until Judge Beatty can hear your case tomorrow. My jail's not too bad. You'll have some great food." The Sheriff sounds like he's apologizing for keeping me.

The cell door's closing, metal against metal vibrates from my fingertips to my toes, my earlier foreboding in the railcar, becoming a reality. Though it's spacious for a prison cell, the room is void of comforts except for a low cot and a toilet. When I sit down on the cot, the blanket and sheets smell freshly laundered. Compared to the last few nights' accommodations, first in the barn, and next in the dirty boxcar, being in the cell warms the cold spot in my soul. I've missed the jail lunch, but the Sheriff assures me I'll have plenty to eat for dinner. Stretching out on the cot to wait, my thoughts become a jumble of worry about Catherine and concern for Gerrit, hoping he pulls through. I hate the guy, but I never intended to kill him.

Before long, the Sheriff opens my cell door to deliver a late dinner. A luscious smell permeates the room. When I uncover the tray I find a meal of fried chicken, mashed potatoes, rolls, green beans, and cherry pie for dessert. My stomach does a flip of joy, and I can't help smiling.

The Sheriff smiles back and shrugs. "I told my wife we have a young man in here that looks like he's hungry, so she made a little extra for you tonight."

"Be sure to thank her for me, will you?" Without saying more, I dive in and stuff myself. After eating, I fall into a deep sleep on the thin cot. Nine hours later I wake to the smells of breakfast food, entirely rested. The drunk in the next cell, groaning and yelling out, hadn't interrupted my slumber. He must have come in during the night, but I didn't even wake.

My yawn is smiled-filled. This jail isn't so bad. At least I get fed well and no more beatings. Will I ever get the past out of my mind? Will I ever be able to forgive Gerrit and Alice? Their sick minds, tainted by their view of the Bible made my life the worst kind of hell. At least now I'm rid of all that, and one day Catherine will be too. I promise myself that.

The Sheriff opens the cell door to carry in my tray filled with breakfast items; biscuits and sausage gravy, coffee, and orange juice, and places it on the end of the cot. The Sheriff says, "Compliments of my wife's fine cooking, made especially for you. She has a soft spot for boys who shouldn't be in here."

"What's going to happen to me, Sheriff?"

The Sheriff's stocky build, large belly, and wire frame glasses remind me of the pictures I've seen of Santa Claus. The VanVleets didn't allow those photos in their home, but I've seen pictures in magazines.

"You'll see the judge a little later this morning, Jed. She'll probably line up some work for you to do around town somewhere, no actual jail time. By the way, it's McCloud, Sheriff McCloud. Most people just call me Sheriff Mac."

My eyes widen at the name Jed, but I remember, the Sheriff has the stolen wallet, so I'll have to make sure I answer to my new name. "What's this town, anyway? I kind of lost track. Those other two guys said they'd take care of getting me west to my aunt and uncle's farm in Nebraska. Guess I never should have trusted them."

"Yep, hope you learned your lesson." Sheriff Mac rubs the back of his neck. This job must get to him sometimes.

"You're in Newton, Iowa. Lots of Dutch people here. Have anything to do with that strange group before?" Mac laughs, and his belly jiggles. "I married a Dutch gal. Lots of rules to live by, but she's a great cook, as you probably figured out."

I keep digging into my breakfast, nod and smile. No point in giving away my past, but I know all about the Dutch Reformed people. Many are great, but then there are those like Gerrit and Alice.

I swallow a mouthful of food. "Am I anywhere near

Nebraska? Like I said, I'm supposed to be going there to help my aunt and uncle on their farm."

"No, you've got a piece to go, but like I said, I wouldn't plan on that any time soon, son. The judge'll probably want you to work off your time for riding the rails before you can move on. Might be a week or longer."

The phone rings in the outer office of the jail. Sheriff Mac locks the cell door behind him and leaves to answer the phone. Is someone back in Indiana trying to contact this office to be on the lookout for a runaway boy or for a murderer? The thought of being found makes my insides churn like an electric mixer. I'm hoping old Gerrit isn't dead, but a lot of blood had seeped onto the barn's cement floor. I've never seen anything like it except when butchering animals. The memory of the bloody scene brings spasms to the back of my throat. I try to put it out of my thoughts and think about other things.

I reason that using Jed's name could be a blessing but also a big mistake. If the judge has the name on the license recorded into the court record and the police in Indiana report the information missing from Jed's body, they could trace it here to me. My hand begins to shake as I shovel more food onto my fork.

Being found out will be a worry for the next two weeks while here in Iowa. All I can do is play by the rules and not get into any more trouble. No matter who they assign me to work for, I make up my mind to stay calm and work hard. I've already worked for the worst person possible. No one could be as ruthless as Gerrit.

It's about ten o'clock mid-morning when Sheriff Mac and his deputy come to fetch me to go to court.

Neither binds me nor uses handcuffs. The guns hanging from their belts are deterrent enough.

The walk to the courtroom involves moving through several hallways and turns, with Sheriff Mac walking ahead with the deputy and myself two abreast behind him. After one more short turn, we come to a large wooden door framed with wide decorative oak trim, completely out of place compared with the stark jail and empty beige-painted hallways. Inside the court, the wood style continues with dark oak paneling on the lower half of the walls and more coffee-colored wood on the half-wall between the judge's elevated wooden bench and the wood gallery benches.

My eyes scan the room, taking in all the finery. My hands begin to sweat, and I rub them on my pant legs. The movement scares the deputy, and he grabs my arm with force.

"Oww! Watch it."

I scowl at the guy with clenched fists but calm down when I hear Sheriff Mac say, "Jerry, no need for that. Jed isn't going anywhere."

Jerry lets go, and motions for me to move toward a long table behind the half-wall.

Judge Beatty is already seated behind her bench. Her red hair and bright makeup make her look clownish, but her dark eyes pierce through the courtroom into my shaky insides. Jerry tells me to sit, and when I do, the judge stares at me for a moment longer before speaking. If her actions are meant to make a person uneasy, it certainly does that for me. My heart begins an abnormal flub-dub.

Finally, Judge Beatty speaks, "Jed Thomas, please stand." She waits while I scoot my chair back, making a loud screech and stand. "You've been charged with riding a railroad car without payment. Besides being very dangerous, it is against the law. Do you understand why you're here?" She stares again, waiting for me to respond.

I answer with what I hope is a loud, clear voice, but my nervous insides make it come out like a scratchy, old gramophone. "Yes, Ma'am. But I only did it to move west as quickly as I could. My aunt and uncle need me on their farm in Nebraska."

The judge's voice has no shakiness to it. "I don't remember asking you why. The reason doesn't matter. You broke the law." Those big, bulging eyes continue to stare.

I drop my head to my chest, my insides trembling like a bowl of Jell-O. All that's heard in the courtroom is the shuffling of papers. The wait makes my breathing as rapid as a drummer's wild strokes. I peek up to look toward the judge.

"Ready to give me your full attention now, Jed?"

"Yes, Ma'am."

"Been studying some options for you. I've had a request from a farmer west of town who needs a field hand. He has some plowing that needs to be done. Think you can handle that?"

Snickers come from the gallery seating, mostly from others waiting to take their time before this judge.

"Yes, did plenty of that before." The judge's eyebrows raise, and she nods her head, making me think there's more to this assignment than she's indicating. I'll do whatever to be able to move west away from the VanVleets. Once I get to this farm, I may get a chance to take off again.

"One week of farm labor." Judge Beatty hits her gavel once, and Deputy Jerry ushers me back out the same door we had entered fifteen minutes earlier. When we arrive at the jail office, I'm left standing before Sheriff McCloud in his office, not locked back up in the cell.

"Have a seat, Jed."

Sheriff Mac picks up the phone to make a call. "Could you run over to Graves' farm and tell him I have his worker ready?"

Sheriff Mac explains when he hangs up. "No phone out there. Had to call his neighbor, so it might be a while."

Chapter 10

April 1961: Tom

Sheriff McCloud studies the paperwork by his desk as I try to get comfortable in the straight-backed chair where I've been told to sit and wait, every muscle in my body as tense as a stone. At one point, I ask to use the restroom, and Deputy Jerry comes in to escort me there. But after that, I'm instructed to sit in the same chair again. At least there's a window where I can watch the traffic drive by on the street.

It's another small Midwest town, but the stores and restaurants surround a square with a massive courthouse in the center instead of one main street. I didn't realize it, but we must have walked under the street to get to the courtroom when I was taken for sentencing. An underground tunnel is a great idea if a real criminal needs to be transported since lots of people walk near the courthouse to do business.

Pictures of the Sheriff's wife and kids hang on the wall along with his academy certificate. Several file cabinets line the wall to the left of the Sheriff's desk, probably containing a file on Jed Thomas by now. I clear my throat several times, but Sheriff Mac doesn't bother to look up.

After a couple of hours, a skinny older man dressed in grubby bib overalls and wearing a ratty John Deere cap shuffles into the office. His ruddy, tanned face and arms carry a layer of dust, so his skin looks almost black. Washing hasn't been a priority for quite some time from the looks of his dirty hands and face.

He nods toward Sherriff Mac. "This the kid?" His voice sounds more like a low growl, making me wonder about my fate working for this man. Will he be as tough to work for as old Gerrit? I squirm in my chair at the thought.

Sheriff Mac gives Tom a long look, then smiles. It gives me the reassurance I need.

"Yep, don't think he'll give you any problem, but you know what to do if he does." He turns to me. "Jed, this is Mr. Graves. He'll be your boss and caretaker for the next week. After that, check in with my office, and you'll be free to go."

I follow Graves out to his old Ford pickup. Rust covers the side panel, and the door groans as I open it and crawl onto the torn seat. The inside smells of chewing tobacco, manure, and sweat, but I don't mind. Anything beats sitting tied to a post in the middle of a cold barn. The ride to the farm takes about forty-five minutes. Forty-five minutes of silence, but it's much better than false preaching and lies.

I wind down the dirty window to get a little fresh air. The earthy smell of new spring growth fills my nostrils and the joy of moving on with my life fills my chest. Trees just starting to bud line this backroad, and spring flowers and green grasses complete the picture along the roadside. The memory of Catherine hunting for spring flowers to make bouquets for our rooms pops into my mind. Would she be out collecting flowers now? Catherine's face the night I left the VanVleets comes to mind. Feeling guilty for enjoying my newfound freedom and calm too much, I plea inaudibly for her safety, hoping God will answer the prayer of a possible killer.

Graves turns into a gravel drive that winds through open fields on either side in need of plowing. "These are a couple of my fields." The low voice scares me, and I turn toward Graves, expecting more, but that's all the old man has to say. Looking out the window again, I make up my mind this will be my life for the next few days. I'm happy to have some purpose. Working will keep my mind off the events back in Indiana.

Stopping the truck in front of a two-story farmhouse, Graves parks where I can take in the scene. The house's former beauty has been lost to long years of neglect. Remnants of lattice trim the roof peaks, and pieces of lattice remain clinging to the trim at the top of the wrap-around porch. The faded siding, not having seen a paint brush on its surface for years, has resulted in graying wood. Missing shingles on the roof beg for repair, but it looks fine to me. I feel as if my life is just beginning.

After exiting the truck, Graves leads me toward the house. "Come on in. You'll be bunking on the back porch. It's a little chilly at night, but I put plenty of blankets on the bed. You can use the outhouse out back and wash up in the kitchen sink. I don't usually worry about that too much during the week but do whatever you want on your own time."

We walk up the rickety front steps, and Graves stops, holds the front door half open, and leans on the doorframe as if he needs to rest before going on. He continues in his low, gravelly voice. "So, you know, if you're thinking about running, Sheriff McCloud's jovial disposition is not an act, but he's got the best tracking dogs around. You won't get far, so may as well make the best of it for the week."

He looks me up and down and motions for me to follow. We walk through the house on our way to the back porch where I'll be sleeping. The interior of the house is a repeat of the house's unkept outside. Unwashed dishes fill the sink, and the threadbare furniture displays stains in unnatural patterns.

"Mind if I use the outhouse?" I don't wait for an answer and make a beeline for the little outbuilding. The outhouse reeks, and some boards look ready to fall off, but I manage my business. The smell keeps me from lingering long, and I hurry back to the house.

Graves watches from the house doorframe leading into the porch, and when the back screen door slaps behind me, he calls, "May as well get started, Jed. Daylights a-wasting."

"About that, would you mind calling me Tom? That's my middle name; my family always calls me that."

"Whatever. Come on out, and I'll get you started with some plowing."

Mr. Graves walks with a slight limp, which I haven't noticed until now. I try to adjust my gait to keep even with the farmer's slower pace across the unmown yard and into the barnyard. I look up with silent thanks for Graves' temperament. No abuse here it seems.

Next to the barn, also badly in need of paint, stands an old John Deere tractor with a plow already attached. I scan the rest of the area. The whole place looks as if care has ended ten years previous. That was one thing the VanVleets had insisted on, keeping the site spotless and as well-kept as their funds allowed, albeit not often being able to afford paint or other supplies for repairs. Maybe with Graves' health condition, he can't manage to fix things anymore.

Graves points to the tractor ready for plowing. "Climb on up there, Tom. Let's see what you can do."

I smile to myself when I hear the familiar name again.

Dirt covers most visible parts, making it look like the dirt and grease have blended into black gunk. Climbing up, my jeans brush against grease mixed with caked soil. Rain may be the only water ever touching it, but it'll take more than rain to clean this machine.

Remembering the steps I learned to start a tractor, I first open the throttle, set the choke, turn on the switch, and push on the starter. The engine fires. Graves doesn't smile, but he slaps the back tire like he's slapping a horse's rump and nods his approval. Climbing up on the hitch bar, the old man rides standing behind me to direct me to the field where I need to start plowing. Graves steps off as I pull the tractor into the first row and lower the plow. Putting the tractor into gear, the old engine grinds but begins to move forward. Graves stands for several minutes watching my progress then turns and saunters back down the lane, surrendering this job to his new hand.

Left to my own devices, I make my way up and down the field rows enjoying the sunshine that warms my fingers and toes until I see the old Ford bouncing along the rutty field road in the early afternoon.

Graves exits the truck carrying a thermos and a brown paper sack. "Brought you some dinner."

"Thanks, it's been a while since breakfast." Graves turns to walk back to the truck without further comment. I would have liked to sit and talk a bit, but he leaves before I can make conversation.

While I work for Graves, the long days of plowing give me a sense of accomplishment, and the quiet in Graves' farmhouse leaves me with a peace I haven't experienced for years. Conversations between us never progress beyond a few minimal statements, but I appreciate the time to think. Graves acts gruff but occasionally there are cracks in that armor. One evening Graves gives me the last of the scrambled eggs, and another time he asks if I'm warm enough on the porch. We settle into a mutual respectful existence, and I begin to relax.

During my week with Graves, I help with other chores around the farm besides plowing. Milking Dottie is my favorite. Most of the time, she's waiting at the barn door when it's time for milking. She knows the routine. Leaning against her flank feels like cuddling with a soft blanket, and my gentle pressure against her side keeps her from kicking into the milk bucket. When Graves isn't around, I talk to Dottie to keep her settled, saying things like. "Good ole girl. You're doing great. Wish I could take you with me."

Holding the bucket between my knees, I grab two teats, pulling down gently as I squeeze. The plink, plink into the bucket wakes the cats, and I give them each a squirt or two. They rub against my legs, begging for more. If only humans could be as easy to deal with as these animals. I long for similar easy human relationships. Graves has been kind, but there's not that close feeling I want and need.

When my week of payback ends, some plowing still needs to be finished. I'm ready to move on but my empty wallet says otherwise, and I don't know where to go. Rubbing my forehead to help with making a decision, my solution is to find some paying work before moving on.

As if Graves has read my mind, he stops me on my way out of the farmhouse when I'm going to town to check in with Sheriff Mac. "I can't pay much, but if you stay and finish the plowing, I'll see what I can scrape up."

"Guess I could do that." Relief floods through me and I offer a slight smile.

Graves drives me to town to check in with the sheriff. Sheriff Mac says nothing about the law in Indiana looking for me, so maybe staying for a while will be okay.

We relax into another week's routine, and I spend most evenings playing with the cats cuddling them close. In the mornings, I gather the eggs and set the basket on the counter.

"Got some nice size eggs today for our breakfast."

Each day, Graves and I work together frying the eggs and bacon. Lunch consists of cold sandwiches, and dinner involves opening a can of beef stew or soup eaten along with large amounts of bread and butter and fresh milk. I try to keep up with washing the dishes, but sometimes I revert to Graves' habits.

After dinner on Thursday, Graves motions for me to follow him out to the front porch. "Let those dishes set. They'll be there next time we need them. Come on out and have a smoke."

We sit in near silence enjoying the spring evening, then turn in early, ready to start the next day again at dawn.

At the end of the second week, Graves hands me an envelope with twenty dollars inside.
"Sorry, I can't pay you anymore. I'll understand if you want to move on, but you're welcome to stay another week."

I stay. I can't help myself. I'm growing fond of Graves the longer I'm with him. The old guy needs help, and this farm lifestyle with no nasty punishments attached makes me feel like a weight has lifted. Graves puts no demands on me beyond farming. He never says much, but when he does, it's usually meant to help me learn more about working on a farm and life in general.

On my last Wednesday, as I drive along on the old tractor, pulling the disk over the newly plowed ground in preparation for seeding, Graves is in the adjacent field planting corn with a newer machine and a four-row planter. From a distance, it looks to me like Graves has stopped the tractor. Something must be wrong with the tool. Maybe one of the planter boxes is plugged up. He often has issues with his old equipment. I make another round, but when I drive closer again, Graves still hasn't moved. There's no one behind the vehicle working on the equipment either. Lifting the disk, I turn my machinery toward the field where Graves' tractor has stalled, wanting to help if I can, my pulse speeding up with the uncertainty ahead.

As I get closer, I see the old man slumped over, his head against the steering wheel. Putting my machine in neutral, I jump down, and run the length of the row toward Graves, afraid of what I might find.

"Graves! Graves!" I call several times. But when I reach the tractor and climb up to try to wake him, I can see it's already too late. The old man's skin is ashen, and no breath escapes from his nose or mouth. My heart clutches inside my chest. This is different from when I found the dead teens. The attachment I feel for the old guy makes my feelings surface and my body shakes with sobs. My voice pierces the morning stillness. "No! . . . No!"

Jumping back down to the soft earth, leaving is my first reaction. Graves owes me for the work this week, so I could ransack the house to see if there's any cash. It wouldn't really be stealing. But I can't leave Graves out here hoping someone will find him, I feel too close to him for that. So, I climb up onto the tractor I've been using and drive back to the farmhouse. Graves has never bothered to install a phone at his place, so climbing into the old pickup I drive to town.

When I rush through the police station door, barely able to talk, Sheriff Mac stops and looks up. His wide eyes and puckered brows show me he knows the seriousness of my visit.

I pace the office as I talk, taking sizable breaths to stay calm. "Got a problem. I think Graves might be dead out there on his place out in one of his fields. You've got to send someone to check."

Sheriff Mac comes around his desk, puts an arm on my shoulder. "Graves has been slowly dying for the last year. Wouldn't take any treatments. Sorry, you had to deal with his time to go. Guess I should have warned you, but thought you'd only be around a week."

I duck out from under the embrace. I shouldn't have let myself become attached. I can't let my feelings affect me again in the future. More hurt will result. I rush out of the office, drive back to the farm, and grab my few belongings and some food. It'll go to waste anyway if I don't take it. Walking backward down the lane away from the farm, tears cloud my vision while scanning the old house and barnyard. I walk toward the highway to continue my way further west.

Chapter 11

April 1961: Tom

After leaving Graves' farm and going back to the highway, I make myself visible to all the big rigs that pass by, hoping some lonely truck driver will want a little company on his way west and stop to pick me up. Ignoring the cars again along the route, I only rush to raise my thumb when I hear the rumble of a turbocharged diesel engine, often indicating a huge scmi-truck meant for long over-the-road trips. Otherwise, I stay well off the roadway, fearing some cop may stop to check me out.

As I walk, my mind settles on old Graves. The guy treated me well. I have no complaints. Graves made sure I had plenty to eat and a place to lay my head at the end of the day without screams and torture. Compared to VanVleet, Graves was a saint. How could it be that I feel genuine emotions for this old man I hardly knew, but none for my adoptive father? It's fortunate I left Indiana. If VanVleet isn't already dead, I know if I had stayed, I would have done the deed as more time went on. The thought of Catherine having to deal with the VanVleets makes my knees nearly buckle. A vision of my sister dealing with old Gerrit clouds my mind. My stomach spasms. I bend and wretch. I promise myself again I'll send for Catherine as soon as I get established in Nebraska. It becomes my sole purpose.

These entangling thoughts block the distinctive sound of a diesel engine until it's a hundred feet away. I charge to a dangerous spot on the road's edge, stumbling over the sharp rim between the pavement and the gravel shoulder, shooting my thumb in the air at the last minute. My momentum pulls me head-first onto the rough berm. Hearing the downshifting of the gears as the huge truck comes to a stop, fills me with relief even though I'm down.

The driver climbs from his raised seat, "You all right? You gave me quite a fright."

He grabs my arm to help me up, but I yank it away. "Yeah, I'm fine. Guess I got your attention, though. Is there room in that big truck for a guy heading further west? I can't pay, but I can listen. That is, if you care to talk."

The truck driver chuckles. "I come from a long line of superb storytellers. Guess it would be nice to have someone to listen. Come on, load up, but no sleepin'. I'm not hauling you along to have the same silence as otherwise. My name's Harvey, but everyone shortens it to Harv. What's yours?"

I hesitate a moment but thinking about the license I carry in my pocket, I reply, "Jed, sir."

We climb into the rig, and I shed my heavy jacket in the warm cab. Harv begins running through the shifting schematic as he pulls back onto the highway. We haven't gone far down the road, and Harv starts talking. Turns out he does have some good stories that keep me from dozing.

"Here's a good story for you. My granddad believed a snake could join back together if cut into parts. Honest to God."

"What? No. Sounds like a great story. I'd like to hear it."

Harv goes on with the story. He says when his grandpa was a young boy, he happened on a snake in the grass. The sudden sight scared him into action, and he began to hit the snake with a stick he carried with him on his jaunts. After several hits, the snake's body split right in two.

"I suppose you're going to tell me that he saw it join back together." I turn to face Harv, waiting for the ending.

Harv smiles, "No, he didn't actually see it, but he returned to tell his dad, thinking he had killed the snake. Then after lunch, he and his dad returned to the site of the carnage, but the snake had disappeared. His dad said he wasn't surprised because a snake could join back together in no time and slither away to safety."

I start laughing so hard my stomach hurts, but when I look toward Harv, the guy only glances my way with a smirk across his face. I get the feeling he believes the story's true.

Quiet settles back inside the truck cab, and the engine sounds become hypnotic, but before long, Harv starts up with another story. Apparently, his family has passed down lots of remarkable tales. I settle back to listen as Harv claims he saw his grandpa chop the head off a snapping turtle.

"My grandpa got that mean snapper to clamp onto a stick and, having a hatchet ready, he chopped his head clean off before that snapper could spit out the stick and tuck its head back into its shell. Then while the head lay on the ground, several nosey chickens who roamed around the barnyard couldn't resist pecking at the severed turtle head."

He pauses for effect and my mouth goes slack waiting for the rest of the story.

"Snap, that turtle's jaws closed on one of the chicken's legs," Harv snorts and laughs at the same time. "I never heard such squawking as when that chicken hopped around the yard with that turtle head dragging behind. Finally, the muscles relaxed, and the turtle's jaws opened to free the curious chicken."

I don't dare laugh this time until I hear Harv let go with a huge belly laugh. "I swear that story's true. I saw it with my own eyes."

Is there this much joy in some people's lives? I have never encountered anyone quite as happy-go-lucky as Harv. I could listen to him twist his tales for the whole ride, but after several more stories, Harv tells me to get some welcome shuteye. Rain starts to pelt against the windshield, and its rhythm makes me fall into a deep sleep.

When I wake, the truck is idling in the parking lot of a small restaurant, taking up most of the room in the lot. The sky has cleared, and a few stars linger in the early morning light from the east. Harv is nowhere to be seen, so I climb down out of the truck and pick my way around the parking lot puddles and go inside to the warmth of the cafe. Harv greets me from a booth next to a window where he sits so he can keep an eye on his truck.

I slide into the booth across from Harv. "Where are we now?"

"We're just outside of Omaha, Nebraska. Sorry, this is as far as I can take you. I need to drop my load and head back."

A waitress moves close and asks what I want to order.

"Nothing, ma'am."

But Harv won't hear of it. "Bring the same breakfast I have. He looks hungry."

Within fifteen minutes, huge plates with bacon, biscuits and gravy, hash browns and fried eggs cover my half of the table. I feel as if I've been given the keys to a brand-new automobile when the waitress sets the huge breakfast down in front of me.

I croak, "Thanks." Tears form at the corners of my eyes. "I can't pay you, Harv."

Harv stares at me. "You know, I don't think the good Lord would look kindly on me if I let you go on your way with an empty stomach. Besides, you were a great listener, and that's worth some compensation." Harv laughs his big belly laugh again and shoves some more eggs and bacon into his mouth.

As I part from Harv, the sun's rays begin peeking through the clouds in the eastern sky. I again thank him for everything, but Harv waves me off and heads to his truck.

I walk in the opposite direction and call out, "When I get ahead, I promise I'll remember what you did and help someone else." That's twice now that I've promised to return some help. I clasp my hands as if in prayer. Someday I'll give back.

Walking further west, I only manage a couple more, short lifts. My feet sting with the constant pounding on the rough pavement, and by late afternoon, my breakfast is only the memory of a full stomach. In the distance, a barn like many of those I've seen on these western farms beckons to me. It's not like the run-down barn full of rats at the VanVleet farm. This barn's bright red paint and straight roof beams make it as inviting as a castle. It's time to settle down for the night.

Chapter 12

April 1961: Tom

I wait in the field out of sight and sit next to a big oak tree in the pasture, watching to make sure everyone finishes their work in the barn before making my move. At one point, I see a large figure exit the farmhouse and walk to the barn probably ready to do the milking. Several cows stand near the barn's rear door, waiting to be let in. Light streams from an open back door, and the cows plod into the barn wanting into their stalls, mooing their approval. I watch the unfolding scene, my whole-body aching for a place to lie down. How much longer before the farmer finishes and heads back to the house?

As I sit on the cooling ground, waiting, the sun's rays shine through the low branches, and daylight flutters away. Birds call to one another and fly to their perches as they prepare for the night. The beauty of nature and the memory of the kind truckers begins to change the emptiness within me, filling it up with joy rather than hate. Shadows grow longer, and soon darkness envelopes me while nodding in silence by the tree. A squirrel chatters up above, and I shudder awake. My head jerks upward. I peak around the tree to see a figure enter the house light's beam, arm's hanging low with the weight of pails filled with milk.

When the glow from the outside light becomes empty of movement, I unwind my tired, achy body and stand, ready to proceed to the warmth of the barn. Moving around the large trunk, the rough edges brush the edge of my cheek, waking me more from nature's touch. Pausing a little longer, I wait another couple minutes, wanting to take no chances. Who knows this farmer's inclination toward a drifter and runaway? Time moves like a sloth as darkness fills the area between the house and barn when the outside light is extinguished.

I creep toward the back door of the barn, the one the cows entered with anticipation to be milked. I feel the same tension but for a much different reason. A place to rest and maybe a little nourishment is all I need. Tomorrow I'll wake early and head further west.

The door creaks like most barn doors do with rusty hinges, and a cat runs to hide. I slide through the slight opening I allow myself between the door and frame. My eyes adjust to the dim glow. The moon's light filters into the barn between some of the dry, warped siding, making shadows on the floor. Walking across the barn, sliding my feet across the cement to keep from stumbling, the cows raise their large heads but continue chewing, ignoring the antics of the intruder.

I make out what looks like a storage bin in the corner. Could my good fortune continue? Shuffling over to it to raise the lid, I find the bin holds potatoes probably set out here to sprout to be used for planting soon. All I care about is filling my empty stomach. Rifling through the box I find several small, firm spuds. Cleaning them and picking off the sprouts the best I can with the corner of my shirt, I return to the stalls.

The pungent, earthy smell fills my senses as I lower myself onto the straw in the corner of one of the unused stalls. Downing several potatoes, I wish for some milk to wash them down, but I'm too tired to check if any cow has more milk to share. I settle down into the dried grass. It cushions my weary muscles, and the cows' rhythmic breathing soon lulls me into a deep sleep.

~

Pain shoots through my leg, but I'm slow to wake. I feel another jab at my leg. Exhaustion has taken over my whole body. My eyelids remain closed. Another shot of pain, this time to my upper arm. Forcing my eyes to open, I rub the sleep from them. This can't be. I wasn't supposed to sleep this long. My plan had been to rest and move on before anyone saw me. The figure I had seen in the early evening rises above me like Goliath wearing a smile.

"Hey, you're sleeping past chore time. If you're going to rent this space, you'll need to pay your way," the big man barks and extends his large hand. The smile disappears, but the laugh lines around his eyes crinkle into a hearty welcome. I grab the offered hand and stand, my legs wobbly beneath me. Now I realize I'm about an inch taller than the man, though much slighter.

Slapping off the straw clinging to my clothes, I look toward the door. "I've got to get on my way. Thank you for the good night's sleep, though."

"Nope. Got to pay the rent first. Go, get those milk

pails over there. You ever milked a cow?"

"Yes, sir."

"Well, get started with Daisy there. She's pretty gentle."

I stare at the man. Is he serious? I expect yelling and being chased off his place, but the giant man acts determined I should earn my keep. The farmer begins his own chores, leading a cow to the milking stanchion, and starts the twice-daily task of draining the precious liquid.

I give up my notion of leaving for the moment and do as I've been told. Shedding my jacket, I grab Daisy's halter to move her to a milking stall, but Daisy has other ideas. She raises her tail, and the smell of fresh manure permeates the barn. I pull harder, but Daisy takes her sweet time, unwilling to move until her business is done. After the cow pile has grown to a considerable proportion, Daisy knocks into me getting to the stanchion, wanting to be relieved of the milk that has filled her udder overnight.

"Make sure you clean her udder good. We don't want that trick of Daisy's to ruin the milk," the giant farmer says.

I manage to get Daisy settled and cleaned, lean my head next to her colossal flank, putting pressure there to keep Daisy from kicking the bucket while I milk her. Holding the bucket between my knees, I grab the teats and pull down as I squeeze, enjoying this familiar chore. Soon I develop the same rhythm as the farmer. Two cats appear, following the sound of the milk hitting the pails. The farmer squirts a little milk toward each, and they spend the next few minutes licking and using their paws to clean their fur of the milk.

"Looks like you have done this before," the farmer says. "After you finish with Daisy, clean up that manure before she goes back into her stall. Try your hand with Susie next." He nods toward the large cow in the stall next to Daisy's. She's massive, like the farmer. In fact, I have never seen a cow quite so big.

After cleaning up the manure and moving Daisy back to her stall, I go through the same routine with Susie. I manage to get her settled in the milking stanchion. But this cow's flank is so tall, I have trouble leaning into her and she manages to kick her foot into the bucket as I milk her. Milk splatters everywhere, and my shirt gets soaked. I look toward the farmer, afraid of what he'll do. I've had experience with ruined milk before and ended up missing meals for a day.

But giant farmer man shakes his head. "That cow is more trouble than she's worth. My fault. I shouldn't have expected you to handle her on your first day milking here."

First day? My eyes bulge from my head. "I can't stay. I need to move on."

"Better come to the house first and get cleaned up. Emily will want to wash that shirt for you. Grab these milk pails, but keep an eye on the one Susie stepped in. Maybe we can strain it enough to use it. I'll let the cows out to pasture."

I do as the farmer says but each step toward the house makes me want to drop the buckets of milk and run. Standing in front of the door, my tentative knock is barely loud enough to be heard. A small woman opens the door and stands there for a moment, unsure of the situation, grabs me by the jacket sleeve and pulls me into the warm, bacon-scented kitchen.

Chapter 13

May 1961: Tom

"**Well, Jacob told** me he might have found himself a helper," the jolly-looking woman says as she guides me to the pantry still carrying the milk pails. The small room feels cool compared to the warm kitchen. The block walls must insulate and keep the temperature cool and even.

"My name is Emily." She motions for me to set the pails on the floor.

I watch as she turns the top to open a large milk can.

"We'll pour this evening's milk into the can for the creamery and early tomorrow morning; their driver'll pick it up on his route to the processing plant." Emily grabs the bucket Susie had kicked her foot into, ready to pour, her arms shaking from the weight.

I raise my voice and try to grab the handle of the bucket. "Don't pour that one."

Emily's eyes widen, and she straightens, setting the bucket back on the floor, waiting for me to explain. Her round face, circled by soft auburn ringlets mingled with gray, shows no sign of impatience, only curiosity.

I hurry to add, "At least that's what the guy in the barn said. Unfortunately, Susie got her foot in that pail, so he said we'd have to try to strain it."

Emily giggles, and her eyes become tiny slits, making her crow's feet more prominent. "Good thing you stopped me. That crazy cow. Always causing trouble. That must be why you look a little wet. Go ahead and pour the other bucket into the milk pail, and I'll set up the strainer."

The door into the kitchen slams. Giant man sticks his head around the entrance of the larder. His lined face shows years of working in the sun. Grayish-blond hair recedes from his forehead making the space above his eyes look as large as a melon now that he isn't wearing his cap.

He smiles when he sees Emily getting ready to strain one of the milk pails. "Great, he told you what happened. We'll have to keep that milk ourselves. Don't want to take the chance of selling it to the creamery."

Once dealing with the milk is finished, all three of us return to the warm kitchen. I lean against the counter, not knowing what to do next, wishing I would have insisted on leaving as soon as I woke. The farmer busies himself by pouring coffee for the three of us and making sure sweetener and milk are added as each person prefers. Emily disappears. When she returns, she carries a clean button-down shirt about my size. The farmer's shirts would be too big, so where did she find the right size so quickly?

"The bathroom's back there if you're shy about

changing here," she tells me. "Leave your wet shirt there, and I'll wash it later."

I want to object, but from Emily's smile, it's unlikely I'll get away with leaving right now. When I return, I see the look that passes between my two hosts. A brief sadness replaces their bright faces, but just as quickly, they both exclaim how nice the shirt looks on me.

"Sit, sit," the farmer says. "What's your name, anyway, boy? You can call me Jacob, and you already met my wife, Emily." He moves closer and puts his big arm around her shoulders. She looks up and beams at him from her small stature, reaching only to his mid-chest.

"Jed, sir," I reply. I scowl at using this foreign-sounding name, but I again need to match my response with the driver's license I carry.

Emily moves to the sink, grabs the towel, wipes the corners of her eyes, and begins frying the eggs and setting the other breakfast items on the table, bacon, toast, and American fries.

I am so hungry I dig into the food as soon as Emily sits down. The other two make no movement towards the breakfast feast. How foolish. I know better. Laying down my fork, I bow my head. Jacob and Emily each grab one of my hands in a circle of faith while Jacob delivers a heartfelt prayer, much different than VanVleet's pious declarations. Jacob thanks God for sending me to them, and Emily gives my hand an extra squeeze before letting go.

I flash a smile toward Emily after the prayer. We eat in near silence, the only sound the scraping of utensils and smacking lips. I try to figure out what gives with these two. How can they welcome a stranger into their home so readily?

The large open kitchen houses a gigantic stove, a refrigerator/freezer combination, and an oversized double tub sink. The chrome dining set includes red check padded seats, backs, and tabletop. A black and white tile floor contrasts with the checkered table covering and painted white cupboards line one wall. The kitchen remains warm with the oil heater chugging out heat and the oven recently turned off. So much so that I become drenched. I fear I may ruin the shirt.

"Excuse me, I need some air." I hurry out the door, slamming it behind me, but I'm unsure what to do next. The cool air hits me like a ball thrown my way, and I flap my arms to dry off. The sun has risen above the treetops, and now I can see how well-kept everything is on this little farm. Everything about the place calls, 'You're invited. Come and stay'. Sitting on the corner of the block wall surrounding the windmill, my thoughts tumble around inside my head. Could I make a go of it here? Is this where I'm meant to be? Jacob and Emily look like they could use the help, and they sure seem nice. I rub the back of my neck while thinking how much I would like parents like Jacob and Emily.

The kitchen door opens, and Jacob comes out and sits beside me. "I know it must seem strange that we want you to stay without knowing you, but Emily usually has a good instinct about people. She's happy to have someone besides me to talk to. Our only son was killed in France in the big war." Jacob pauses and sighs. "She gets a little lonesome out on this farm. Emily was a town girl, so the solitude's been hard for her."

I stay silent, not knowing what to add after this

disclosure. The windmill turns making a creaking sound as the spring breeze picks up.

After several minutes, Jacob stands and faces me, his back a little bent from years of work. "Why don't you come in again? Maybe you don't need to move on as quickly as you think. I sure could use the help this spring with the planting and other chores."

Jacob extends his hand to me. After a few seconds, I return the shake. "But you don't know me. I could be a bad guy."

"Emily trusts you already; like I said, she has a good sense of people. 'Course that doesn't mean you won't have to prove yourself. It's hard work on a farm, but I promise we'll treat you fairly. You must have worked on chores before, judging from your milking skill."

I only stare at Jacob. There's no way I will let him know anything about my past. What if Jacob has connections in Indiana? I won't ruin my chance of staying away from that place. Getting Catherine from there will never happen if I'm sent back before I'm ready. And if Gerrit is still alive, no one will believe the stabbing was an accident.

Jacob goes to the door and beckons me back inside with a smile and slight wave. I get up and follow.

Emily stands and gives me a quick hug. "I'm so glad you decided to stay."

I sit to finish eating but give no comment, my eyes focusing on my food. I can't let myself get attached to these people.

For the rest of the day, I help the old farmer with whatever chores must be done. My confidence and self-esteem return when Jacob praises me each time I complete a task. Emily prepares a lavish spread of ham, mashed potatoes, and several sides at lunch. I've never eaten such good cooking, better yet than the Sheriff's wife's cooking.

Afterward, I help Emily clear the table without being asked, and her smile spreads to a large half-circle. Jacob and I rest in their living room for a while before returning to work. Jacob's chair sits opposite a small console TV, a green couch with rope trim fills another wall, and another rocking chair faces the TV on the other side of the couch. A large school clock hangs above the sofa, and the mantle holds many photographs of their son as a toddler to his days in uniform. Maybe staying is going to be too weird after all. I don't want to be a substitute for this young ghost. Tomorrow I'll leave after I've worked off their kind help.

When it's time to turn in for the day after the evening chores and meal, Emily says, "I've made up our son's bedroom for you. I think you'll be comfortable there."
I shake my head in denial. "Nope, can't do that." Grabbing my jacket from the back of the chair, I hurry out of the house to the barn before either of my hosts can stop me. Jacob follows, but his older legs aren't as fast. He arrives at the barn as I struggle to open the heavy door.

Jacob motions for me to step aside, "Here, let me show you. There's a trick to opening this old door. Lift as you pull."

He demonstrates, and the creaky door swings open, allowing the sweet smell of hay to fill our senses again. He grabs my arm before I can move inside. "Come back to the house, Jed. Emily will be so disappointed."

I pull away and stand my ground. "I'm not your dead son. The barn will do fine."

Jacob's smiling face turns to stone. "Have it your way. I'll wake you in the morning in time to help with the milking. The old outhouse is behind the house if you need it."

Chapter 14

May 1961: Tom

For the next week, whenever I mention leaving the farm, either Emily or Jacob come up with some chore they need me to help with. I hate to disappoint them, so I continue to stay.

When I help Jacob fix the stubborn barn door, he slaps me on the back and says, "I couldn't do it on my own. I needed someone strong to hold it up while we put on the new hinges."

Emily bakes me some cookies when I spend an afternoon cleaning out the gutters. She laughs and says, "Maybe now we won't have grass grow in those gutters anymore. Jacob and I haven't been able to climb that ladder lately."

I can't say no to any of it. Jacob's encouraging words and jolly disposition make the chores fun and Emily's gentle words melt my heart. I tell myself if I continue to sleep in the barn, it's not a permanent arrangement so I won't feel bad about leaving them soon because I need to move on. This jittery feeling never seems to disappear. Every time a car approaches on the road past the farm, I check to see if it's the police.

However, the couple's actions toward me and each other do make me wish I could stay. Words of love are not often spoken between Jacob and Emily, but how they treat each other shows how much they care for one another. The couple's joy in everything they do gives me a pattern to live by, and their love makes me hope for a relationship like theirs someday for myself. When we settle in the kitchen for a meal or spend the evening in the living room, I find myself nearly bursting with good feelings. Before, only Catherine could make me feel this happy.

At breakfast on Sunday, Emily reminds us that this is a day of rest, and they will be attending church in Greenwood. "Why don't you join us, Jed? We could introduce you to some of the other teens."

"Nah, I'm not too much for church."

Instead, I ask if it would be okay if I went fishing. With the Mulders gone, it will be a great time to make a break for the road west.

"Suit yourself, but you'll be missing a great potluck after the service," Jacob says. "Emily made her famous German Potato Salad. My family's Dutch, but I married a good German girl." Jacob lets out one of his hearty laughs, and the look between the two is like winning the lottery.

"Oh, Jacob, Jed doesn't care about our courtship." Emily turns back to me. "We'd love to have you come with us today, though. It's a wonderful time to get to know some folks."

"Maybe some other time, Ma'am." Looking at

Jacob, I ask. "Mind if I take one of the cane poles in the shed to do a little fishing?" My afternoon plans must be convincing, so the Mulders will believe I'll be here when they return.

"No, no problem. We'll see you later. We usually get back to the farm about two o'clock if there's a potluck after the service."

Emily and Jacob set the dishes in the sink for later and hurry to finish getting ready. I begin the task of washing the dishes.

Emily calls out as they walk out the door, "There's plenty of sandwich makin's for lunch, so help yourself. You leave the rest of those dishes and enjoy yourself."

I follow them outside and wave as the old Chevy heads down the gravel drive and onto the highway. I hurry back to the kitchen and finish washing the dishes for Emily. Grabbing some lunch meat and bread, I stuff them in one of Emily's sandwich bags for lunches. There's a thermos on the counter, so I fill it with fresh, cold milk. Leaving the inviting kitchen, I pause to scan the room. Leaning against the door jam, my breath catches, I sigh and turn to exit.

Walking toward the highway, the birds' songs and early morning sunshine pulls me to a path
along the pasture instead of turning right toward the road. By using this farm path to get to the next farm driveway, I'll be able to intersect with the highway and be on my way west again.

The warm sun slows my walking to a stroll, and my eyes are drawn to the clouds that dot the sky here and there like dandelion puffballs ready to burst forth. I grab a stick to poke rocks and old stumps along the way. My step slows to a turtle's crawl. The Mulders won't be back until two, and I've made up my mind to be long gone by then, but I may as well take in nature along the way. Alongside one stump, a patch of morel mushrooms catches my eye. I'll have to tell Emily about them so she can cook them for dinner. Wait, what am I thinking? I'm not going to be here later.

The cows graze in a shady spot on the other side of the fence from where I walk. All eat contently twenty feet inside the pasture fence except for Susie. The fence wire sags as ornery Susie cranes her neck across the wire for that grass that looks greener on the other side. I place my lunch on the ground, shoo Susie away a few steps, and lift one area to try to straighten the old wire. But the brittle wire snaps, and now a gaping hole causes the fence posts to lean away from the center of that section.

Susie sees her chance and hurries through the gap to that supposed better pasture grass. I try to grab her halter but miss. She takes off running and kicks up her heels, trying to play a game. Susie hides behind a little sapling, twitching her tail as if to say, 'come and get me.' I walk toward her, with my hands behind my back. Being smarter than a cow becomes my goal. But each time I get close, Susie takes off and runs out of my reach, far away from the safety of the pasture.

The hole in the fence is my main problem right now. I need to find something to plug the
break, so the other cows won't get out. Wanting to leave but knowing I need to fix the fence so Jacob doesn't have more work, my stomach becomes a jumble of knots while trying to decide.

Finally, my decision made, I turn back toward the barn to find something that might work as a barrier.

Running at the speed of a hummingbird's wings, I hurry back to the barnyard. Along the side of the old hog pen is an iron hog panel about six feet by four feet, built like a fence with cross wires welded together at intervals. *Perfect.* Now to carry it back to the broken wire, get Susie back inside, and be on my way. I enter the cool of the barn to find something that might be the ticket to help catch Susie. Hanging on the wall behind the door are lead ropes, each with a clip to attach to a cow's harness.

As I return to the broken section, Susie still stands outside the fence, munching away where I left her. I lean the hog panel up against the standing fence section next to the gaping hole, so I can slide it shut quickly behind the ornery cow when I get her corralled. I move toward her now, holding the lead rope behind my back. She watches me advance, tail twitching and those big eyes staring my way. I try walking sideways, turning my head so as not to make eye contact, but as I come close, Susie runs a few feet away again. This happens three more times, and I'm about to give up. But I know I'm more intelligent than a cow. I grab a huge handful of the new grass she likes, and I hold it to my mouth, pretending to eat it.

Susie gets interested. Without waiting, she lumbers over to where I'm standing, and I get my chance to snap the clip to her halter. The click of the lead rope startles her. Susie takes off in the opposite direction from the opening in the pasture fence. I hear the saying in my head, 'Never let go,' so I hang on. I run along and keep up until Susie races right for the creek. She stops at the water's edge, and I tumble down the bank into the water, where I sit, still hanging onto the lead rope.

"Shoot, cow! You'll keep me here on this farm even if I don't want to stay."

I scramble out and up the bank and yank on Susie's rope, grabbing handfuls of grass to entice her as we walk back to the pasture. Once Susie is inside again, I place the hog panel back across the opening and wedge some large dead branches against it to brace it for the night.

Walking back toward the creek, lunch in hand, my boots sloshing with each step, I sit on the bank to eat. A sob comes from down in my toes and knocks the feelings loose inside of me. What am I trying to prove? The Mulders are the best thing that has happened to me in a long time. Why can't I accept that this is where I'm supposed to be? Maybe I can make a new life here with the Mulders. Getting up and wiping the stinging tears away, I slosh back down the path towards the farmyard.

As I enter the barnyard, the Mulders are exiting their car and begin waving their welcome. I wave back but stop, my intentions still wavering. Emily opens the car's back door, and a black and white Border Collie bounds out, running straight for me. The dog bounces and barks until I bend down to greet it.

"Who's this?" I ask, confused.

"One of our friends at church couldn't take care of Charlie anymore. We think every boy needs a dog, so we stopped by on our way home to get him. That's why we're a little late," Emily chirps.

"What happened to you? Did that big fish pull you into the creek?" Jacob asks, smothering a laugh.

My breathless answer makes Jacob break out into a smile. "Susie got out of the pasture when the wire broke. I tried to get her back in, but she

stopped right before going into the creek, and I
didn't. We'll need to fix the fence tomorrow. I think it
will be okay until then."

Emily grabs my arm. "You come in the house, and
I'll get you some dry clothes, and I won't take no for an
answer."

"Yes, Ma'am," I say. "But I'll need to hurry. Jacob
will need help with the milking later."

Chapter 15

May 1961: Catherine

For a few days after returning home from the hospital, Gerrit had remained quiet, either sitting in his favorite chair in the living room or resting in his bed. Gradually things return to the same arrangement as before the incident. Gerrit again does the outside chores and along with the work, his mean temper returns.

I try to stay away from him, fearing the worst while going about my chores and doing my homework. At night I read until I fall asleep and then get up and start the same pattern the next day. Will my life ever have any joy again?

No one mentions Tom. It's like he never existed. Occasionally, I hear someone at church inquire about him, but the VanVleets always answer with, "He doesn't live with us anymore." Why isn't someone looking into his disappearance? I only want to know if he's safe. He's the only family I have left.

I lie in my bed, trembling, after another episode of scolding and beatings for supposed failed chores. With

Tom gone, it's my job to kill the chicken for Sunday dinner. Today it took me so long to work up the nerve, Alice had to come out and do it herself. Her yelling could be heard for miles. "You lazy girl. What's taking so long? I need to get the chicken to frying so it will be done when Gerrit wants to eat."

When Gerrit hears the commotion, he plods into the back yard. "When are you going to learn to do what you're told?"

He grabs my arm and holds me close before beating me, making sure he touches my breast. He stares into my face with those small, beady eyes making me wonder what's going on in his head. His putrid breath almost makes me gag.

"Bend over that stump." He pulls his belt from its loops, and I scream even before the belt makes contact. Three times it hits, but after the first, I stay silent.

When he finishes, Alice yells, "Get inside and dress this bird."

As I walk toward the back door, my backside feels numb, but I won't let them know it hurts.

Most days I try to stay close to Alice, but sometimes there's no way I can. Some mornings before Alice wakes and Gerrit is supposed to be getting ready to milk the cows, he climbs the stairs and stands in the doorway of my bedroom. I can feel his stare, and my body stiffens. I pretend to be asleep, and so far, he's left without incident.

Now that Tom is gone, Gerrit yells at any little thing that sets him off. Maybe because he's left to do most of the work himself. He yells at me to do the chore over again or gives me more work. So far, Gerrit's only grabbed me or kicked me. I hate the man.

Will I go to hell for the way I feel? I ask God for forgiveness each night, but the next day the same feelings return when I see him again.

Bruises cover my body, but when I attend church or school, I'm told to wear my long skirt and a sweater to hide my arms and legs. No one suspects and no one questions why I often stay home from school. The term is almost finished for the year, and graduation is right around the corner, so the teachers don't bother to check. Hoping to be allowed to go through graduation, I work extra hard so the VanVleets will let me join the rest of my class in the ceremony.

At the end of May, the VanVleets decide we should attend our church's annual picnic. Alice tells me, "I expect you to sit with us for lunch and the afternoon missionary service, but after that, you can join the other teens for the softball tournaments and other games. Make sure you behave."

I've never been allowed to mingle much except at church or school. Fear grips my insides when I'm allowed to wander. Walking with my head down toward the game area, I stand by myself, watching the activity. Using the back of my hand, I mop away the perspiration that has developed on my neck and face. I see a group of popular girls from my church standing on the edge of the game area. If only I had the nerve to join them.

"Hey, Catherine, want to be my partner in the sack race?" I turn and lower my eyes when I see it's Roger, the guy who sits behind me in algebra. He twists a burlap sack in his hands and waits for me to respond.

I answer without looking up. "Guess so." I feel myself heat up from the inside out and sweat trickles down my armpits. Gerrit and Alice haven't said I can't join in the games, so maybe it will be okay.

"Come on, the race is getting ready to start." Roger grabs my hand, and we walk, swinging our linked arms to the starting position.

Getting into the gunny sack becomes challenging, especially for me since I'm wearing a dress, and our giggles break the tension. Finally, we each have one leg in the bag, and we're lined up with the rest of the contestants on the starting line. The starter yells, "Go," and Roger and I begin to hop and run. Our movements make us destined to win.

"We're ahead. Keep it up," yells Roger.

But Roger's foot swings wide and catches against mine. Tumbling to the ground, my dress flies up, and I catch a glimpse of Gerrit VanVleet staring at us from the sideline. His scowl makes me want to run away and never come back, but Roger stands and pulls me up. Catching my eye, Roger smiles and my heart flutters inside my chest.

Roger helps me get my leg back inside the bag. "Come on, let's finish. We're a good team even if we might come in last."

After the race, Roger guides me to the refreshment stand, and we pick out sodas. A man from the church dips his hand into the horse tank full of ice and sodas and hands one to each of us. "Enjoy."

We saunter back toward the game area. Sitting close together on the ground, we watch the rest of the events with Roger doing most of the talking. I will not let Gerrit ruin my afternoon, so I concentrate only on what Roger is saying. At one point, he slips his hand into mine, and I feel my heart thud against my chest. Could my future include having a boyfriend someday? Right now, I can't imagine how.

Later, when we return to the farm, Gerrit catches me as I exit the car. "What do you think you were doing, playing around with that kid? Haven't we raised you better than that? Showing off your underthings in that race makes me sick. Go up to your room. I'll be up later to deal with this."

I do as I'm told but my insides become mush. I watch from the window and see Alice head to the barn to do the milking. The sound of Gerrit's heavy steps climbing the stairway makes my head pound. I turn to see his wild-eyed expression as he stands in the doorway, reaching for his belt. I cringe in the corner making myself into a ball.

Gerrit pulls his belt from the belt loops and slaps it into the air. "Bend over here on the bed."

When I don't move, he steps closer and grabs me and throws me onto the bed. My dress tears open with the rough handling to expose my chest. Time strings out like the sound of windchimes in the distance as he stands there, staring down at me. I try to pull the fabric together.

Gerrit's pants fall to his knees. He doesn't try to retrieve them. A low growl emits from his gut as my fingers fumble with the buttons. The belt drops from Gerrit's hand. He climbs onto the bed and shoves himself on top of me. My screams are unheard as he pulls down my panties and forces himself into me. Scratching at his face and neck becomes my only defense until he manages to hold my arms still and finishes his deed.

The rest of the summer, each time Gerrit asks Alice

to do the milking because he doesn't feel well, and I'm supposed to be starting dinner, the routine is the same, except the couch or a table becomes the means to his end. He warns me not to make a sound, so I hold it in along with my screams of hatred. Those I keep inside myself until the day when I, too, can escape.

Each time Alice returns, dinner isn't ready, and she berates me for my laziness but helps me finish, anyway. It's as if she knows what's going on. My longing to leave this place grows more each day.

Chapter 16

July 1961: Tom

By the end of July, I've become acclimated to the work on the Mulder's farm. Though I refuse to sleep in their son's room, I spend more and more time inside with the couple. The evenings fall into the rhythm of cleaning up the dishes after dinner, showering, watching a game or show on the black and white TV, or reading. The Mulders always read a passage from the Bible after their evening meal, and I sit and listen to be polite. But so far, I haven't agreed to attend church with them. They've not pushed it, which makes me appreciate them even more.

The fields of corn and soybeans that Jacob and I tilled and planted have grown to near maturity. Since the work on the farm has decreased a little, I spend every free hour roaming the area with Charlie always by my side. That dog is the best thing the Mulders could have done for me. I love being able to talk to him. He's a great listener.

Walking along the creek has become our favorite

jaunt. Charlie runs ahead, hunting squirrels or rabbits and barking at the base of a tree or a rabbit hole until I call him off. He runs back to me and looks to me for approval. I kneel and rub the back of his ears. "Good dog. You're such a good dog."

The VanVleets had not allowed us to have any pets, so the connection I enjoy with Charlie makes my heart swell with a special kind of pleasure. I feel like there's a balloon inside my chest waiting to burst each time I spend time teaching him a new trick and Charlie achieves it.

Today as Charlie and I walk, he begins barking wildly at whatever is under a rock near the creek. When I catch up, I hear the distinctive rattle of a massasauga rattlesnake.

"Charlie, get back. Leave that snake alone."

But Charlie is too agitated to listen to me this time and keeps barking. The snake responds with more warning rattles. Charlie attacks, and the snake recoils for a moment. Jutting its head forward to take a bite out of the dog, Charlie jumps aside just in time, but keeps barking.

This dance continues with Charlie bouncing in for a bite and the snake retaliating with a
strike. The snake makes a final attack, but this time Charlie gets to the opposite side of the snake and grabs it behind its head. Just as he's done many times with his rag toy, Charlie shakes the snake, tail and head section flinging back and forth. Guts fly as the dog's teeth dig deeper through the flesh. I jump aside to keep from getting sprayed, fearing the worst, that Charlie might have been bitten.

"Charlie, drop it," I yell several times, a command

the dog knows from playing fetch. Charlie stands over the snake, panting, his fur full of guts and blood, looking to me for praise.

"Good dog, Charlie, you saved me." I pet an area of fur free of debris, trying to hold back my tears of concern for Charlie. "Come on, we need to wash you up and check you out."

When we return to the barnyard, I relay the story to Jacob, gasping out my shaky words. My heart races with concern for Charlie.

"He's acting okay," says Jacob. "Maybe that snake didn't get in a good bite."

Together, we manage to get Charlie in the horse tank to wash him. Though he often goes into the creek, bathing him in a water tank becomes a war of wills. Jacob holds his collar while I suds up his body and rinse him off with the hose. After lifting him back out of the tank, Jacob and I stand back while Charlie shakes the water from his fur.

I rub my hands through his hair. "Can we take him to the vet to make sure? It will cost, but I've been saving most of the money you pay me each week. I'll use all my savings if I have to. I want to make sure he's okay."

Jacob slaps me on the back. "I like the way you're showing your love, kid. Dry him off, and we'll get going."

We pile into Jacob's old Ford pickup with Charlie sitting like a wet king between the two of us. Before long, Jacob and I crank down our windows halfway to eliminate the wet-dog odor wafting from Charlie. The warm breeze does its job of drying the dog, and I continually rub my hand over Charlie's back.

Jacob glances my way. "Ever have a pet before? You sure have a knack for handling this dog."

I stay silent. I don't want to break my rule about not giving away my past. I don't know what Jacob would do if he knew what I'd done before I left Indiana, and I don't want to think about that either.

"Okay, I get it. No questions. But I hope someday you'll feel safe enough with us to talk a little about your past."

The silence continues for several miles as I pet Charlie to keep him calm, the landscape changing little. Fields of corn and soybeans line about every mile along the highway, all soon turning from bright green to ugly brown, the cycle of growth complete.

"No," I blurt out after another quiet mile. "Never allowed to have a dog."

Nothing more is said. This tidbit is enough for now. The truck's motor chugging along as we drive the rest of the way to town becomes the only sound filling the cab.

When we arrive at the vet's office, I lead Charlie into the reception area, occupied by only one other dog and its owner. Charlie can hardly contain himself with the excitement of seeing another dog and proceeds to stop halfway across the tile floor to poop. The lovely smell permeates the sitting area, and the young receptionist notices my plight.

"Don't worry. It happens all the time."

She comes around the counter with paper towels, a dustpan, and a spray bottle. The girl's blond hair falls past her headband as she bends over to clean up the mess.

She looks up and flips her hair back in place just as

Jacob enters after finding a parking spot. "So, Sarah, guess you met Charlie and Jed already." He laughs as if this is the funniest thing he's ever seen. Charlie sits by my side, head down.

When Sarah stands and smiles at me, I stammer a soft explanation. "So sorry. He's never ridden in the truck this far before. Guess he got a little nervous. Plus, he had an altercation with a snake and had a bath, things he doesn't usually have to deal with."

"Let's get him checked in. My dad will examine him for you, don't worry." She returns to her area behind the counter and writes Charlie's information in their logbook as Jacob and I answer her preliminary questions. In a matter of a few minutes, Sarah comes back around to take Charlie back to the exam room.

"Can I come, too?"

Sarah's face lights up with another smile looking right at me. "Sure, it might keep him calmer."

I follow along as if I'm another puppy. I turn to see Jacob sitting back and smiling to himself.

After a complete exam, Charlie receives a clean bill of health from Sarah's dad. I pay the bill and thank Sarah for all her help but not meeting her eyes. Heat rises to my forehead and butterflies fill my middle during the whole exchange. I've never spoken to girls much, especially one this pretty.

On our way back to the farm, after we've been driving a short way, Jacob says, "Sarah's kind of cute, isn't she? I think she likes you."

I cannot stop smiling. My lips feel stretched as if pulled both ways by strings. Knowing Charlie is okay and meeting Sarah makes the hard truck seat feel like a cloud. Sarah's pretty face keeps flashing before me. It seems like she might be interested, but how can I reciprocate when I need to move on soon.

"How do you know Sarah?"

"Oh, we've known her since she was a little girl. She and her family go to the same church we attend. I think she'll be a senior at the high school here in town this year."

Pondering this news, the rest of the drive, I whistle a tune as we bump along. When we arrive back at the farm, Charlie bounds out of the truck to chase the chickens like usual. They scatter, and he runs back to me for approval.

"Looks like he's back to his ornery ways," Emily says as she joins us in the driveway.

~

Ever since the vet visit, I've been fantasizing what it would be like to be able to get to know Sarah better. My head tells me it can't work out, but my heart says otherwise. Why shouldn't I be able to have some happiness? But that question won't be answered until I know for sure whether Gerrit survived.

My heart wins the battle. On Saturday night, I ask Emily if she has any nicer clothes I could borrow. On Sunday morning after chores, I surprise her by dressing in them after my shower and announce before breakfast that I would like to attend church with them.

Chapter 17

July 1961: Tom

On the way to church, I squirm in the Chevy sedan's back seat, and not only because of the tight collar and tie. The lie about my name must be set straight before either of the Mulders introduce me to their friends. I roll down the back window, hoping the cool air will align my thoughts into straight truths like the fence posts that pass by as we drive.

Emily turns to face me. "You're pretty quiet back there. Don't worry, everyone is friendly."

I slap the back of the front seat as if needing attention, my voice pleading. "Got something to tell you and can't explain right now. It's too long of a story."

Jacob and Emily glance towards each other, concern a straight shot between them.

I go on, worried what the Mulders will think, "When you introduce me, could you please say my name is Tom instead of Jed? I promise I'll tell you the whole story later. It's too long to go into right now."

Jacob snickers. "Going to be confusing for us, but I guess if you've got a good reason, we'll try to keep it straight."

I settle down as Emily begins singing a familiar hymn along with the car radio. After a few more miles, Jacob turns into the parking lot next to a small white-sided building with one high-gabled section in the middle. A large walnut-stained wooden cross is mounted in the center of the gable. A low-roofed addition off to one side, topped with a much shorter gabled roof makes the building look little lop-sided. I had imagined a brick structure like the reformed church the VanVleets attend. Hopefully the service will be different, too.

Jacob parks the car, and before entering, someone calls out, "Hello." Jacob responds with a wave and a return greeting. I note the friendly atmosphere immediately. On entering the church, no one is seated and quiet. Instead, everyone mills around, talking before the service, some carrying coffee. The little kids run from one another, darting in between the legs of the adults, only getting reprimanded when they run into someone. The high-beamed ceiling and linoleum covering the floor instead of carpet, make every sound in the meeting area echo like being in a canyon, but no one seems to pay attention to the extra sounds.

Jacob takes me over to a group of men standing near the back entrance of the church. "Want you to meet the young man who's been helping me out on the farm this summer. Finally convinced him to join us at church." He smiles and gives me a wink. "This is Tom. I suppose if he decides to stay around, he'll be attending school with some of your kids."

My knees nearly buckle. I'm not thinking about going back to school. In fact, I figure I'm done with it for good. But I manage to hold it together and grab the extended hand of one of the men in the circle who looks familiar.

"I'm Sarah's dad. At least that's how all the kids refer to me. Also known as Dr. Werner. I'm the veterinarian that treated your dog, Charlie. How's he doing, by the way?"

"He's great," I say, still holding the guy's hand. "Is Sarah here?" I look past Mr. Werner to scan the room.

"She'll be along. Her friend, Nathan, is picking her up for the service today. I think he hopes to be more than a friend." Dr. Werner winks and looks around the group, and chuckles.

My insides turn into a soggy dishrag. I should have known a girl as friendly as Sarah would have a boyfriend or many boyfriends. Other men in the group offer their hands and say their names, and I try to be attentive, but their names escape out the window as soon as the men share them, my thoughts only on the girl.

Loud talking catches my attention at the entrance. Several teenagers walk in, Sarah among them. Her light blue dress compliments her cornflower blue eyes, and her blonde shoulder-length hair is teased and sprayed to perfection today. When she notices me, she waves and smiles. I nod, but my mouth remains as tight as a sealed envelope.

The pastor and the council enter, and the organist plays a hymn. Everyone joins in singing as they move to find a seat. Now with the organized music, the acoustics work their magic, and the singing sounds like little choirs all around the room. I sit next to Emily but notice when I peek toward the back, the last rows on the opposite side of the church fill with young people sitting separately from their parents.

The pastor's message on forgiveness gives me something to think about, and I catch some of the sermon. Pastor Jenkins's delivery is easy to follow, but my thoughts drift off, wondering about the girl on the other side of the church. As a result, I only remember some of the message. The hymns are familiar, ones I sang when I went to church with the VanVleets, but the organist plays them with gusto, and the singing here is joyful, not solemn.

When the service ends, Emily pulls me over to meet her friends, and the ladies make comments about how good-looking I am and what beautiful brown eyes and dark hair I have. Considering most of the people here have either blond or auburn hair, their comments make me realize I do stand out.

"Mrs. Mulder, are you ever going to introduce your helper to me, too?"

I turn to see Sarah standing right behind the group of women, so close I can smell the toilette water she uses after her shower. She smiles again and says, "We met at my father's office, but we've not been formally introduced."

Mrs. Mulder turns toward Sarah and puts her arm through hers to pull her closer to me. My
breath catches, and my tongue feels like an inflated balloon in my mouth. Why does this always happen when talking with girls?

"Sarah, this is our friend, Tom. He's been such a big help to Jacob all summer. We do hope he stays on for a while." As she says this, she slides her arm through mine, and the three of us stand connected like links in a chain.

"I do, too," Sarah says, looking into my eyes. "So, it's Tom, now? Thought your name was Jed."

"Long story. Maybe I'll tell you sometime." I look away, unable to meet her stare, my stomach full of little moths beating their wings against my insides.

Sarah changes the subject. "How's Charlie doing?"

Emily gives my shoulder a light tap as she turns back to the circle of women she had been talking with. I manage to get my voice back a bit and bark out, my eyes now inspecting my shoes, "He's good, ornery as ever, no more snakes, lately."

"Maybe I could come out to the farm one day, so I could check on him, sort of a follow-up visit." Sarah steps closer, but I take a step back.

"I don't think that would be such a good idea. What's your boyfriend going to say about that?" I still don't look at Sarah's face. Can't she see she's making me uncomfortable? I start to walk away.

Sarah's voice rises to a high crescendo. "I don't have a steady boyfriend. Who told you that?"

Talking stops in our corner of the church for several seconds. The eyes of all the close parishioners fall on us. Sarah grabs my arm and guides me out the side door of the church. The warm summer breeze does little to cool us down, and we shade our eyes from the bright sunshine. I grab Sarah's hand and pull her toward a giant oak tree near the edge of the parking lot, but we stand staring into each other's eyes, at a loss for words once there.

Sarah looks down at our hands still entwined.

"Sorry, I made a scene in there, but I didn't want to let you leave without knowing the truth. I would like to visit the farm sometime." She stares at me, trying to gauge my reaction, but lowers her lids when there's no response. "Oh, forget it. But why are you still holding my hand if you don't like me?" Sarah tries to break contact, taking a step toward the church.

It's as if I finally wake from my trance. "No, wait, Sarah. It's just, I can't believe you want to spend time with me. I'm a nobody and I may not even be staying around here."

Sarah returns to stand close. "Oh, I'm pretty sure you'll stay." She smiles, and her blue eyes sparkle with mischief. "I'll come out to check on Charlie on Tuesday."

Sarah's parents exit the church, and I drop my hold on her hand. She runs to her ride home in the family car. Striding over to meet Jacob and Emily as they walk toward their car, I feel as if little clouds lift each step I take.

Chapter 18

July 1961: Catherine

The hot summer months drag on for me. My upstairs bedroom has little ventilation, and the warm nights give no relief for my constant nausea. I feel awful most of the time. Remembering how Mom felt before she told us she was having another baby, makes me wonder if I'm in the same situation. By the end of July, I've missed my period for two months. I don't have any menstrual rags in the laundry, and I vomit in a bucket every morning before going down to breakfast, so I'm sure Alice is suspicious, too.

She watches my every movement. When I run from the dinner table to lose the fried chicken I've just eaten, Alice sends me to my room. I slide down under the blanket when I hear footsteps on the stairs, dreading the thought that it might be Gerrit. Someone yanks the sheet back from my face. Thankfully, it's Alice who stands looking at me for several minutes before she speaks. "Have you been letting the boys have their way with you?"

"When?" I yell. "You never let me out of your sight. You know whose baby this is." I turn away expecting a swat, but angry words come instead.

"You little slut. We never should have taken you and your brother in. It's only given us pain and heart ache. First, Tom tries to kill your father and runs off, and now you're pregnant. What will the church think? How will we explain this?"

Now heavier steps ascend the stairs. Gerrit walks in, and I point at him. "Ask him. He knows why I'm in this condition. He did this to me."

Gerrit's eyes dart from Alice to me like a trapped animal. Finally, he yells, "You're no daughter of mine. You'll be making your own way after this."

I turn toward the wall. I should have left with Tom. Now it's too late.

~

Neither of the VanVleets speak to me for the next month. I stay in my room as much as possible, only coming out to do the chores I'm required to do and attend church, trying to pretend all is well. The morning sickness subsides somewhat but my appetite does not return. Lying on my bed, I rub my belly and smile as I imagine the baby there, but visions of Gerrit's face on the child make me want to gag. If only Tom would come back for me, maybe we could run away again together. I don't blame him, though. He has no way of knowing what has happened to me.

At the end of September, Alice helps me pack up a few belongings. She also gives me a couple of her large dresses to pack for the trip. "You'll need these soon enough."

I don't dare ask what is going on. Tears are at the

surface of my eyes during the whole ordeal. Within the hour, we're in the car and Gerrit is driving us away from the farm and heading north with the only sound inside the car, our heavy breathing.

Alice turns to me in the back seat once we're on our way. "We've found a nice home in Michigan for unwed mothers."

My spirit soars, but I don't comment, afraid they may not follow through. Anything will be better than staying with the VanVleets.

After driving three hours, Gerrit turns into the driveway of a rambling old house set back from the road with a spacious yard and the greenest grass I've ever seen. The gravel driveway crunches under the car's tires as we pull slowly toward the broad steps leading to the wrap-around porch.

"Remember, you got pregnant by a neighbor boy," Gerrit says, looking straight at Alice as he says the words.

Alice glares back at him but only nods. "We won't take you back with a baby, so you may as well make up your mind to give it up for adoption. That will be the best for everyone. You can come back to the farm when this is all over."

I don't reply. I'm never going back there.

Gerrit opens the car door. "Okay, if this is all understood, let's go in and get you settled."

The three of us exit the vehicle and walk up the broad steps. I take in the beautiful flower plantings in front of the porch and the red burning bushes planted at each corner. If I didn't know my future involved carrying a baby to term, this would be a dream place to vacation.

The director meets us in the hallway, giving her name as Miss Dawson, and Alice introduces everyone in our group. Miss Dawson calls for a young woman about my age whose belly looks ready to pop.

"This is Jenny," Miss Dawson says. "She will be your roommate until she leaves in about a month. At that time, she and her baby will return to her parent's home, right Jenny?"

Jenny nods but doesn't say anything, not looking at our little group. Taking me by the hand, she leads me down the hall. Neither of the VanVleets says good-bye, and I don't turn around. I have no reason to want to see them ever again.

Chapter 19

July 1961: Tom

The busyness of the day keeps me from bringing up what I need to explain about my name to Jacob and Emily. Finally, after eating dinner and devotions, still seated at the table, I begin to tell my story, slowly getting the words out between sighs and deep exhales.

"Suppose I better get to the point about my name. Thanks, by the way, for introducing me as Tom without any questions." I stop to take a breath and look from Jacob to Emily. They nod their approval. "Tom is my real name. Tom VanVleet, but I don't like the VanVleet part. I'm adopted. I left that life one night after being tied to a post in the barn for several days, and I'm not going back."

Emily's eyes fill with tears, and she grabs my arm to reassure me. Silence fills the kitchen, the only sounds, the birds' chirping outside the open windows and Charlie's loud breathing on the kitchen floor. I struggle with the shakiness inside before saying more.

Jacob takes another drink of his after-dinner coffee. "You don't have to say anymore now, Tom, if you don't want to."

"No, you deserve to know what kind of person you have staying here." I take another deep breath and go on. "That night, VanVleet came out to the barn to make me apologize after I had been tied up several days. When he cut me loose, I grabbed the knife, and there was a skirmish." I break down into silent sobs and cover my face. Seconds tick by like the movement of a sloth. Jacob hands me his hanky and Emily squeezes my hand. I take a deep breath and continue. "I didn't mean to do it, but he fell right on the knife, and I was so scared, I ran. I don't know if he died or what."

Jacob and Emily both rub my arms now, encouraging me to go on. "It sounds like it was self-defense, Tom," Jacob says, speaking in a near whisper. "Maybe running was not the right thing, but being tied up like that has to have some bearing on your actions, too."

"It wasn't the first time." I keep my eyes down. I don't want to see if there's disappointment in their eyes.

"You've not shown me any kind of behavior while you've been here to warrant that kind of punishment." Jacob shakes his head and stretches, rubbing the cuffs of his shirt at the corners of his eyes.

I rub the tears from my eyes and blow my nose, a welcome sound, and the tension breaks. "That's because you laugh and show me how to do something better, where VanVleet would yell and get angry when I messed up. That time all I did was ask for the gravy because I said the roast was a little dry."

Emily slaps her head. "Oh, my, if I punished you

every time my cooking didn't turn out, we'd never get anything done around here." Laughter breaks through the tightness that had been squeezing at our chests. Thinking my story is about finished, Emily gets up and starts to clear the table. "Well, I'm glad that's off your chest. We won't need to mention this again unless you want to."

"No, wait, there's more." She sits back down and places her hand back on my arm. I go on. "When I left that night, there was a terrible accident. Two of the star basketball players from my high school got in a horrible wreck. I found them soon after it happened on my way out of town. They were both dead. Well, the one died as I held him. It was awful." My shoulders slump, and I hold my head in my hands, elbows propped on the table. Taking another huge breath, "That was so hard."

Again, Emily rubs my arm. Seconds pass before I can go on. "I didn't know them well
because I was never allowed any activities outside of school, but it was still awful. I wasn't thinking straight. I figured the police would be out looking for them and me before long. All I wanted to do was get out of that town, so I grabbed the one kid's wallet and took out his driver's license and some money. I've been passing as Jed ever since, but some guys I met stole the money." I look from one to the other. "That's another whole story for another day."

Jacob gets up to pace the kitchen, stops at my chair and places his big hand on my shoulder. "We're here for you, no matter what. I've not heard anything in your story that makes me want to turn you into the authorities. But if you'd like to know how this VanVleet fellow is, I have some family in Indiana that I could call. If he's as mean as you say, he probably survived a little knife wound."

I sit up straight and dare to smile a little at Jacob's words. The tight spot between my shoulder blades starts to relax. I give Jacob the name of the town I left and the church the VanVleets attend.

Jacob's eyes widen at this information. "Some of my extended family live in that town in Indiana. It won't be difficult to find out what happened and how Gerrit is doing."

After clearing the dishes and cleaning up the kitchen, Emily takes both of my hands in hers and asks me to look at her. "Tom, considering your experiences with staying in barns, I think it's high time you start spending nights in the house. I've been packing away all our son's memorabilia, so it will be your room now."

I can't help myself. I grab Emily and give her a huge hug. Perhaps there is a God who's watching over everything I do. But I'll be more convinced of that after we receive word about VanVleet's condition. That night in the soft, warm bed, I pray again for Catherine's safety.

On Monday, I elaborate on my story when Jacob and I are in the barn milking and cleaning the stalls. "I didn't want to say this stuff in front of Emily, but I have a sister who is still with the VanVleets that I'm concerned about. She's eighteen, and I don't like how the old man looks at her if you know what I mean."

Jacob stops scooping the straw and stares at me. "I'm so sorry you and your sister had to go through this. I don't understand how some people can act so righteous and be so evil."

"Catherine, that's my sister's name, told me the VanVleets came and got us in Chicago when we were little because our real parents couldn't afford to keep us. But all they wanted was for kids to do their work. It was ten years of pure hell for me, excuse my language." I pause and look toward Jacob, squinting with hatred. I realize my gaffe and I change my face to a smile. "Oh, I know that's what I've been doing here, too, but it's different. You give me lots of free time and make it fun to do the work. And I feel like you and Emily actually care about me."

Jacob laughs that endearing hearty laugh again and returns to cleaning the stall. "That was quick thinking on your part. Yes, we do work hard, but I can tell you don't mind, and I like how you're eager to learn. In fact, after Labor Day, even though I need help getting in the crops, I'd like to see you go back and finish your schooling. You can still help me after school and on Saturdays."

I start to object, but Jacob cuts in, "I know it's not your top priority, but think about it. As for Catherine, I will find out how we can get her out of that house. I'm planning on making that call later today, but it's going to be difficult approaching the subject without giving away the fact that you're here with us."

Quiet falls over the inside of the barn as the two men work. The cows' soft chewing and snorts as they're moved from their stalls to be milked make the day seem normal, but thoughts move like a cyclone through my head. I don't want to go back, but if it means keeping Catherine safe, I guess I might have to. I blurt out, breaking the stillness, "If I have to, I'll go back."

"That's the last thing I want, Tom. I've been thinking. I'll call my cousin Joan. She's always got the latest gossip. She'll probably give me what I need to know about the VanVleets before I ask because I'm sure it's big news in that town. I can ask her if they have any kids, and I'm sure she'll tell me all about you and Catherine. I think that will work."

Right after lunch, Jacob calls his cousin, and I can tell from his face, he's getting the information we want. After the call ends, Jacob says, "Joan said the whole town's talking about where the son could be after beating up on his father like that. She also said, VanVleet survived the attack. He needed to spend several days in the hospital, but he's doing fine."

I breathe a sigh of relief. At least I'm not a murderer. It's like a hundred-pound weight has been lifted from my chest. I plop down on a nearby chair, afraid my legs won't hold me.

Jacob goes on to say he asked if other children are in the family, and Joan shared that no one has seen the daughter around for a while. Jacob stops to look my way for a moment and goes on with faltering voice. "Joan said everyone wonders what's going on in that house, but no one dares check."

When I hear that, I can't help it. I stand and take out my anger with a kick at one of the kitchen chairs. It falls to the ground, but I do nothing to right it. Instead, I run from the house, needing some space. Charlie whines at the door, but I hurry outside without my buddy.

Chapter 20

July 1961: Jacob

When Jacob goes to do the evening chores, he half expects Tom to be waiting in the barn, but there's no sign of him. His bent and weakened frame displays the loss, while moving around the stalls. Will Tom come back on his own? The most he can do is hope and pray.

"Susie let's ask God to take care of Tom. Remember how he saved you when you got out of the pasture? Now let's pray that God will save Tom and bring him back to us."

Susie turns her head to stare at Jacob as he continues to milk her and prays with a loud, anguished voice, raising the rafters with his thunderous prayer, sounding more like he was yelling at God than praying. "God, are you testing us once again? Please bring Tom back to us. He needs more help and guidance. Don't write him off as hopeless."

He and Emily lost their only son to war. He had accepted that, after time, as God's will, but losing another loved one would be more than the two could endure. When Jacob finishes the tirade at God, the plink, plink of the milk hitting the pail is the only sound in the barn. No critters dare to intersect with Jacob's anguished movements.

As he trudges toward the house, both arms hanging low carrying full milk pails, the cool night air refreshes his spirit like a cool spring rain. He stops and glances up at the starry sky, and again wonders at the majesty of his God. But when he enters the kitchen alone, with the buckets of milk swinging from both of his hands, Emily's downcast face stings him like an arrow piercing his heart. She doesn't question; she goes about their regular routine. Without speaking, she grabs one of the pails from Jacob and plods to the larder to deal with the milk. Jacob's eyes meet hers again as he pours the milk from one of the pails into the large milk can, almost missing the opening. He knows they have become too attached to the boy. He's a drifter, not their son, and that may not change even with all the love in the world.

However, still hoping Tom will return, the Mulders stay up until their eyelids begin to droop. When the clock above the couch chimes ten, Jacob stands and rubs his eyes. "Bout time to turn in. He's not coming back tonight."

They toss about after retiring, listening for any slight sound that might indicate Tom has stolen back inside. Both unable to sleep, they lay holding hands, saying silent and audible prayers for Tom's safety.

Morning comes earlier than usual. It's still dark outside when Jacob flops his feet over the side of the bed. "We may as well get up. Maybe turning on the kitchen lights will signal to Tom that we're eager for him to come back."

When Jacob heads to do the morning chores, he turns on the lights in the barn and scans the open stalls for Tom. He had hoped the boy would return to his former sleeping place, but that empty feeling returns when Tom isn't there. Jacob does the milking on his own, talking to the cows the whole time in a prayerful litany, not raising the rafters as he did the previous night. Where could Tom have gone? Had he headed back to Indiana to finish the job on VanVleet?

Entering the kitchen alone, Jacob sees Emily's hopeful expression sag once more. They go through the motions of eating breakfast, clearing the table, and washing the dishes with only a few necessary conversation exchanges. Jacob grabs the dish towel and dries the dishes, lately a job Tom has been doing. At different moments, they bend down to pet Charlie to reassure him that he hasn't been forgotten.

Charlie paces from one end of the kitchen to the other. Several times he stops and whines by the door even though Jacob has already let him out twice since he's been back from milking.

"Can't believe he didn't take Charlie."

The dog, hearing his name, trots back to the couple for more petting.

"Makes me wonder if he'll be back soon. Wasn't Sarah supposed to come out to the farm today?" Emily's soft voice trails off as she bends down again to rub Charlie's ears, talking to the dog, not expecting an answer from Jacob.

Jacob sits down to read the morning paper. The dishes clatter as Emily begins to store them away, then the room falls silent except for the wind whistling through the half-open old window sash. Emily stands by the sink, looking toward the barn through the window, saying a prayer for Tom's safety. She says to no one in particular, "That wind sure is picking up. Hope there's no storm today."

A soft tapping soaks through the quiet, but equal to the sound of loud banging because of the stillness within. Neither inhabitant moves.

Jacob comments, "Probably a branch hitting the siding because of the wind."

Louder repeated rapping on the wooden door makes Jacob look up from his reading. He glances at Emily, but she seems unable to move. Charlie rouses and steps closer to the door, beginning a deep guttural growl. Putting his paws up on the screen opening of the door, he yips, and whines. His tail begins to wag like a sail in a windstorm.

Jacob stands and hurries to the door. The rumpled image of a teenage boy greets him through the screen. "Tom, what are you doing out there knocking? Get in here so Emily can get you some breakfast." He pushes the door open, but Tom doesn't make a move inside.

Charlie bounds out and jumps up to greet his person. Tom pushes him away, but Charlie won't be put off. He rubs against his legs and Tom relents and gives him a slight pet.

At the sound of Jacob's voice, Emily wakes from her trance and hurries to get into the scene. She steps out and gives Tom a hug. "We were so worried about you. Where did you spend the night? Nights are starting to cool down. You've got to be freezing. Come in and get cleaned up and I'll fix you some breakfast."

Tom waits for a minute after Emily's prattle. "I can't accept your goodness again. I messed up leaving the way I did. I'll be out of your way as soon as I get my things."

"Nonsense. You'll do no such thing." Emily grabs his arm and tugs at him to follow her into the kitchen as Jacob holds the door open, and Charlie continues to jump around, barking at the unlikely trio. They stumble over the loose threshold and move into the kitchen, laughing at the dog's excited antics.

Jacob slaps him on the back. "We want you to stay, son."

Tom can't help but smile at the kitchen's familiar aroma and the Mulder's warm welcome.

After he takes a shower, Emily has his breakfast ready. Sighing, he looks from Jacob to Emily, and down at his hands as he says, "I'm sorry about how I reacted to the information you found out, Jacob. I'm so upset about leaving Catherine that I wasn't thinking straight. Sorry, too, that I missed the evening and morning chores. Make sure to dock my weekly pay. I'll try to make this up to you if you want me to stay."

"We understand how difficult it is not knowing how Catherine is doing." Emily pauses and squeezes his hand. "Where did you go, Tom? It had to have been an awful night."

"After riding west in that rail car, sleeping in that old, abandoned Chevy on the next farm over wasn't too bad. Someone left an old horse blanket lying on the back seat. Comfy, even if it was a little smelly."

Jacob laughs. "No wonder Charlie went nuts when he first saw you."

Tom runs his hand over Charlie's soft back. "You mean it wasn't because you missed me, ole' boy?"

Jacob takes his dishes to the sink. "I'm not sure Charlie knew what to think. Without you,
he's lost. He tried to jump up on our bed last night. But, of course, Emily didn't want anything to do with that, and she sent him packing back to your room."

My eyes widen, and a smile spreads from one ear to the other. *Your room?*

Charlie jumps up to look through the screen door again, and his loud barking would make anyone come to attention.

Emily peeks out the kitchen window. "Oh, I believe it's Sarah. With all the excitement, I forgot she was coming today."

Tom's smile is as broad as an open door.

Jacob laughs. "I think that's why you came back. You didn't forget Sarah's visit out to the farm today, right? Don't worry. We'll keep your secret."

Chapter 21

August 1961: Catherine

I soon learn why the girls' home looks immaculate. Each girl is assigned several daily tasks, either cleaning, pulling weeds, doing laundry, or helping with the food preparation. I don't mind. I'm used to hard work. The September weather remains hot, but I look forward to my chance to work outside. Today, my roommate, Jenny, and I are assigned to dusting and mopping.

"What should I do, Catherine?" Jenny stands in the middle of the hallway holding the feather duster.

I take Jenny's hand and together we swipe the duster over the top of the entry table, then the tops of a few picture frames.

"That's all it takes, Jenny. Just go around stuff and over the tops of things. Now, I'm going to mop the floors while you keep dusting."

Jenny moves from room to room using the feather duster while I man the mop and bucket. The sweetest voice tinkles through the halls and falls on my ears. At first, I think someone has turned on a radio, but the singing stops for several seconds, then begins again, much softer. When I turn the corner, I bump into Jenny and the music stops.

"Jenny, you sing like an angel."

"That's what Kevin said. He was my boyfriend, but Mom and Dad don't like him." Tears form in her eyes and looking down, she rubs her large belly.

I give Jenny a hug. "Hey, we don't need boys. You stick with me. We'll figure it out together."

I try to be a caring friend to Jenny, and Miss Dawson praises me for my help. Just now, she steps from her office and smiles at the two of us as we embrace.

After I got settled that first day, Miss Dawson met with me. She explained that Jenny is a special case. "She doesn't go to school because she's considered a slow learning. Her cousin took advantage of her naïve nature, and she ended up here, pregnant."

My situation isn't much different, except Jenny loved the attacker, whereas my baby came from hate.

All of us girls at the home meet with the nurse once a week and a doctor once a month until the last two months of our pregnancy, when the visits are increased to twice a month. We also are required to attend a group session once a month.

At night after dinner, Miss Dawson and another counselor meet with us individually to discuss anything we want to talk about. Our options are presented. If we decide to give up the baby, they explain that a family is chosen to take the infant when it's born. Some girls, like Jenny, keep their baby with their family's help.

They also are required to attend a different group session once a month.

When it's my turn to meet with Miss Dawson, she praises me. "Thank you for being such a caring friend to Jenny. I see how well you work with her each day. I'm so thankful for your help." She gets up from behind her desk, comes around and joins me on the other side of her desk.

I sit looking down at my hands. "She's so sweet. It's easy to be nice to Jenny. Being with her has made me realize I want to do something to help others. I never had a chance before to think about what I want to do with my life."

In one of the group sessions, Mary, another resident at the home, from Indiana, breaks down as she shares how she became pregnant by her mother's boyfriend. I feel tears forming, but I'm not ready to share yet. I have to get away from this discussion, so I stand suddenly and run to my room, Jenny follows not far behind.

"What's the matter, Catherine?" Jenny holds her swollen belly, out of breath from running,
but as she waits for me to answer, she grabs herself as water trickles down between her legs onto the floor. "No, I didn't mean to pee," she cries.

I run into the hall. "Help, I think Jenny might be going into labor."

There's a flurry of activity as the nurse arrives with a wheelchair, Miss Dawson packs Jenny's belongings, and soon I sit alone in our room, wondering how Jenny is doing and what my new roommate will be like.

Chapter 22

August 1961: Tom

No matter how many times Emily tells him to shush, Charlie doesn't stop barking, so I push open the screen door for him to rush out to meet Sarah. She opens the car and climbs out as Charlie bounds toward her, knocking her back into the driver's seat.

I watch the scene and call Charlie back. Waving, I hurry toward this girl I hope to get to know better. Today her hair is tied back in a ponytail, with fluffy teased bangs falling low, hiding those blue eyes I like so much. She's dressed in a pink T-shirt and jeans, along with white sneakers, maybe not the best choice for a farm visit.

When I approach the car, Sarah remarks, "Guess Charlie's fine. Maybe I made a trip for no reason."

I drop my head, and my smile disappears. "Thought maybe you came to see me, too," I mutter.

When I look up, Sarah's broad smile reminds me of a bow on a package and just as pretty. She continues to smile letting me know she's joking. "Nope, Charlie is my only concern today. I think we should take him for a long walk and make sure he's alright."

"Sounds like a great idea to me."

Jacob and Emily come out to greet Sarah. She hugs them both. "How are you guys doing?"

They respond positively, but then the silence intensifies. I stand with my hands in my pockets, bouncing on my toes several times. Sarah plays with the gravel in the driveway with her foot. Still, no one speaks for several seconds.

Jacob turns to walk away. "Come on, Em, these kids want to get on with their visit. I'll help you pick a few tomatoes for lunch."

"More like you'll watch me pick, you mean." Emily jabs Jacob with a little punch in his side, and then says to Sarah, "You'll stay for lunch, won't you, Sarah?"

I catch her eye, and, from her slight smile, I know she wants to stay. "Well, I need to get back to my dad's office, but maybe if we eat early, I can get back before the afternoon appointments."

"Sounds like a plan," Emily says.

When Jacob and Emily leave for the garden, I start down the path toward the creek. "Let's go find a squirrel, Charlie." Stopping to look at Sarah, I say, "You coming?"

Sarah smiles and laughs. "Thought maybe you were only inviting Charlie." She moves toward me as I shake my head.

Two separate paths have formed from the movements of tractors and other equipment heading toward the fields. The grass and wildflowers make a strip of green between the sandy lines. Charlie bounds ahead of us, as we walk side by side but a couple feet apart.

Often the path turns to mud where a puddle hasn't dried, and at one of these spots, Sarah crosses a little closer to me, trying to keep her sneakers clean. I see my chance and catch Sarah's hand. She doesn't comment but squeezes back enough to let me know it's okay.

We saunter along as Charlie runs ahead and circles back to check on us.

"Charlie looks like he's recovered just fine," Sarah comments.

"Yeah, not that there ever was anything to be worried about, but I'm sure glad we took him for a checkup. Otherwise, I might never have met you." When I steal a look at Sarah, she's smiling but looking down.

More trees line the farm road, enclosing it so walking through it is like entering a whimsical tunnel. The warm August sun causes sweat on our brows, but neither of us suggests turning back. Instead, our concern is for one another. At first, our conversation is full of questions like, what's your favorite food, do you have a favorite book, how do you like working at the vet office or on the farm?

Sarah asks, "Where's your family, Tom? Do you have any brothers or sisters?" The silence becomes deafening. My hand tightens on hers. Stopping, she turns to look me in the face. "Sorry, I didn't mean to upset you."

"I ran off last night," I blurt. "I wanted to go back to Indiana to take care of my sister, who still lives with our adopted parents. I'm so worried about her, but right now I need to trust Jacob's advice."

I pull Sarah closer needing comfort and sense her longing to fall into my arms, but she holds back. It's too soon for this type of closeness.

The wind picks up, and a few early falling leaves blow between us. Pulling away, laughing, Sarah wipes the leaves from her shirt. Black clouds have begun to roll in above and block the sun. The temperature drops in just a short time.

"Maybe we better head back," Sarah says. "That sky looks pretty dark."

"Yeah, guess so."

We walk back, single file this time. I hang behind, wanting to kick myself for making that move too soon.

"You can tell me about your sister if you want." Sarah stops and kisses me on the cheek.

"Maybe another time."

Charlie comes racing around us, then running back to the barn as if crazed. I shrug. Drops begin to fall on the top of my shoulders and head, and I understand Charlie's hurry.

"Beat you to the barn," I yell.

I run backwards for a few feet to make sure Sarah follows. That action gives Sarah the chance she needs. She streaks past me, and I puff along to catch up and stay even. The rain comes down harder. Grabbing Sarah's hand again, I race towards the barn door, smiling to myself at maybe getting a second chance to steal a kiss.

Since the repairs, the barn door opens with little trouble. We fall into the safety of the warm space, laughing and bending to our knees to catch our breath. The summer storm sounds like pounding nails above us. The beating rain on the barn's roof means no leaving for a bit.

I look around for something to use to dry off. An old towel hangs by the milking pail, not the cleanest, but it will have to do. We wipe our faces, necks, and arms. Sarah hugs her body, and I notice her shiver though the temperature inside the barn is as warm as a kitchen on baking day.

The lingering smell of the cow's distinctive odor combined with the sweet smell of new hay sends me mixed signals. Sleeping here in this barn has become a safe harbor from those meaning to harm, but other memories of barn experiences are not so pleasant. I push them back into my head and concentrate again on Sarah. She shoves aside her carefully styled bangs and lifts her arms to wring the water from her ponytail. Every movement gives me more reason to gaze, but when I notice her wet t-shirt clinging to her body, I look away, embarrassed for staring.

We stand uneasy for several moments, listening to the rain pounding on the wooden shingles above us. After several minutes, I pull her to the corner, where I lift a bale of hay, trying to make a sitting area to wait out the storm.

As I toss it behind another bail. Sarah screams, "Behind you."

A giant rat sits in the middle of the floor, stunned by its sudden discovery. Sarah runs to the wall and grabs a long-handled hoe. She lifts the hoe and charges, meaning to scare the rat toward the door, but I move in the wrong direction into its path. By this time, the confused rat runs at me and heads up the leg of my jeans. Dancing around and shaking my leg, I try to oust the intruder. Looking at Sarah, who stands watching my antics while shaking with laughter, I give a final big kick, and the rat flies through the air and comes close to hitting Sarah. The laughing stops, and a high-pitched scream replaces it. The poor rat runs for its life and burrows under the hay in one of the stalls. I grab the hoe from Sarah and smack the piles in a wild frenzy until the rat lays in a bloody heap. Picking it up by the tail, I fling it out the barn's back door.

Stunned into silence by my aggression, Sarah sits on the bale, exhausted. I join her. Neither of us speaks for a moment.

"I hate rats."

Sarah looks straight at me. "Yeah, I figured that out. That was a little over the top."

I don't respond. The sound of the rain subsides.

Sarah says, "Maybe we should go in for lunch."

"I had to keep the rats away by staying awake," I share, holding my head in my hands. My body begins to shake next to Sarah's and she places her hand on my thigh.

"He would tie me to a post and leave me there for days. The rats would come out at night. That's why I hate them so much. Sorry, you had to witness that."

She doesn't ask for more explanation. I rest my head on her shoulder. She holds me until my breathing slows and the shaking stops.

Chapter 23

August 1961: Tom

Until the second week of August and fair time in Nebraska, I spend as much free time as I can with Sarah. We meet at church, sit with the other teens, and afterwards, walk around the grounds and talk. Sarah drives out to the farm on days when she isn't working at her father's vet office. Often, she helps me with my chores, or we go fishing or hiking around the property with Charlie at our side.

Occasionally, I'm allowed to borrow Jacob's pickup to visit Sarah in town. Emily instructs me, "Now you be polite and go to the door when you pick her up. You want to make a good impression."

Sarah never invites me in. She's always ready and waiting when I knock. On those days, we ride around the back roads and Sarah points out where each family lives that attends our church. Sometimes we stop for a picnic along the roadside if time allows.

If I am working on fixing a piece of machinery for Jacob in the old shed, Sarah hops up on the tool bench and watches, occasionally asking a question or handing me the tool I need, but mostly we're both happy to spend time together, not always needing words.

As Sarah sits there watching, one day in early August, she brings up a touchy subject again. "I hope you'll make up your mind to go to school with me in September. Then we can see each other at school, too."

I don't see myself as a student. I try to explain why I don't want to go. "I never did very well in school. Not sure I want to finish. Besides Jacob needs me here."

Jacob and Emily keep talking about me going to school, too, but I clam up when they suggest I return. How will Jacob get by if I'm at school the whole day?

I'm beginning to feel like a racehorse trapped in its stall. The restless feeling won't go away and at night I often can't sleep. We still haven't found out how Catherine is doing. Jacob's cousin says no one in the town knows what happened to her. If it wasn't for Sarah and the Mulders, I would be on my way back east to find her.

Thankfully fair time in Nebraska helps me focus on other events besides Catherine's whereabouts. Not that I will ever forget. Thoughts of her linger in the back of my mind like a tiny block of ice that never melts. But the excitement of looking forward to the fair activities and preparations on the farm for the fair week help me to concentrate on them instead of Catherine. Emily prepares her strawberry jam to enter for judging, and Jacob decides to register Susie into the dairy cow class judging.

"Tom, since you've got practice getting Susie to do what you want, I think we can handle getting her in the stock wagon, don't you?" Jacob pats me on the back and laughs. He's as excited as a little kid thinking about the blue ribbon, he thinks Susie will earn.

I'm not so sure. I try to get Jacob to face the facts. "Susie does what she wants. I wouldn't count on her behaving while at the fair."

However, Jacob's mind is made up. On Monday of fair week, Jacob borrows a stock trailer from our nearest neighbor and pulls into the barnyard honking the horn. "Get in the truck and back the trailer up to the barn door, Tom. We'll trick Susie into thinking she's going into another milking stall."

Getting Susie to the fair is the easy part, it turns out, and Susie does as Jacob hopes, coming away from the judging with a blue ribbon. The rest of the fair week goes well, too, and Sarah and I have a ball enjoying the food, animal judging, and carnival rides. But on the last day of the fair, some kids set off fireworks near the judging tents, and Susie goes wild.

"Grab that cow!" yells someone as I walk back to the judging area with my hotdog in hand.

People scatter and zigzag from the open door of the arena, followed by Susie, running in a frenzy as if unsure of where to go next. I drop my food and make a beeline for that crazy cow. When Susie sees me, she runs in the opposite direction, away from the crowd. I manage to get close enough to entice her the way I did in the spring when she escaped from the pasture, grabbing handfuls of grass and holding them for Susie to eat. When she takes the grass, I get close to her, and pull on her halter attaching a lead rope.

Jacob yells from a livestock trailer not far from where I'm standing with Susie. "Bring her over here. We'll load her up and get her back to the farm before she does any more damage."

I pull as hard as possible, moving Susie halfway to the trailer, where she decides to stop. I bend over to catch my breath, and my hands burn from the rough rope. Another hand appears from behind me on the cord.

"Maybe I can help."

A third farmer slaps Susie on the rump, shoving from behind, and we three manage to get her into the trailer.

Jacob thanks both men, and I hurry for the truck's passenger side, ready to leave.

"We could use a kid your size on our football team this year," the one guy says. "I'm Mr. Robins. I coach the football team. We're already practicing, but we can use another strong fella."

Standing by the truck's open door, I look to Jacob to explain that it won't be possible, but Jacob only smiles. "It's up to Tom. We can probably make it work."

"I'll have to let you know, Coach."

I hop into the truck, brow furrowed. Now I'm not sure what to do. I'd like to tell Sarah I'll be joining her at school, but how can I leave Jacob without help?

It's as if Jacob has read my mind. "Don't you worry about how we'll get things done if you go to school and play football. I've done the work myself before and I can do it again. Besides, my friend, Cal, just retired from the hardware store and he's always bugging me to come help on the farm.

I shake my head. I can't talk with this lump in the back of my throat. It seems everything is falling into place for me.

After delivering Susie back to the barn's safety, Jacob says, "Let's hurry and do the milking, and go watch the tractor pull. Got to return this stock trailer I borrowed anyway."

When I meet up with Sarah in the grandstand, I can't contain my excitement. "Guess I might be joining you at school after all and not only that but I'm going to be playing football besides."

I expect a celebration, but Sarah grows quiet.

"What's the matter? I thought you'd be happy."

Sarah shrugs it off, but still stays quiet. We watch the unfolding tractor pull for most of the evening in near silence, enjoying our elephant ears and lemon shake-ups.

"Let's go get some actual food. I'm starving," Sarah says. "Maybe we can find a place a little quieter, too. We need to talk."

I follow her out of the grandstand, but she doesn't give me her hand. She stops near a large oak tree in the shadows far away from the midway and grandstand noise. She kisses me long and hard.

"I know you said you were hungry, but I didn't know you meant for this," I tease, a little breathless, chuckling. Trying to begin another kiss, I move her against the tree trunk, holding her arms back. Exploring her mouth, I seek out her tongue when she parts her lips.

Not trusting myself, I pull back. I stand facing Sarah, not touching her. "What gives? Just because I'm going to be with you at school, now you're anxious to make out more?"

Sarah stammers, "My parents have been on my case. They want me to break up with you. And now that you'll be so busy, they'll get their wish. You won't have time to see me."

I ignore that part and zero in on the words, 'break up.' "Is that why you've never asked me to come into your house? I didn't know they didn't like me. They hardly know me."

Sarah's head falls to her chest, and her arms cross as if for protection. Tears glisten in her eyes when she looks back into mine, reflecting the midway lights. "I'm sorry, Tom. I should have told you what's been going on at home. Most of the time, when I'm with you, I've made up excuses saying I'm going to a girlfriend's or shopping or something. My parents know I've been seeing you, but not as much as we've been meeting."

I take several steps back and raise my voice. "That's crazy. I can't help what's

happened to me before, but I'm trying to make a new life here with the Mulders. That's got to count for something. And now that I'm going back to school ..."

Sarah cuts in and tries to touch me, but I take another step back. "Yes, when I heard that, I was so relieved. That's been one of my parents' arguments for me to break up, that you don't go to school. So now they can't say that anymore." She moves closer to me. "Let's go back and try to forget all this. I'm sure my parents will come around now."

"No, I don't need to prove anything. If that's how your parents feel, we don't need to continue this." I walk away toward the parking lot leaving the one person I thought I could always depend on.

Chapter 24

September-November 1961: Tom

In the fall of '61, my senior year, life becomes a roller coaster of football practice, school, and work on the farm. I love the busyness, and Mr. Robbins turns out to be a great coach. At first, the schoolwork is a challenge, but Emily sits with me each evening and helps me catch up. By the end of the first quarter, my grades become acceptable.

Now I only see Sarah in passing at school and if I go to church with Jacob and Emily. But lately, I'm often choosing to sleep in on Sunday morning and instead I take Charlie out for a run. It breaks my heart to see her with the other guys at church, so the less I go, the better.

~

After the season's last football game, a group of us players hang out at the corner drive-in, celebrating our win. I settle myself in the midst of them, wanting to be part of the group. Sarah's car makes several circles around the block, but I try to ignore her and her friend,

Karen. The other guys notice and yell invitations each time they go by.

"Hey Sarah, come on in and join our little group."

"Karen, tell your friend to pull in next time you go by."

Whistles taunt them to stop. Sarah and Karen wave but drive on by. My heart does a flip. I would have loved to have the guys talk about my great game in front of Sarah.

After the girls drive away, Jerry says, "Come on, let's blow this joint. We've got some better stuff out by the lake."

I start to follow the team to Jerry's truck but stop, walk to my borrowed truck instead, and yell back, "Hey, I'll follow you guys to the lake. It's on my way back to the farm, so I'll save miles when it's time to leave."

Beer flows with abundance after we reach the picnic area, and my head spins after a couple cans. I haven't had much experience with drinking and visions of the night I found the wreck before I left Indiana knock around in my head. I sure don't want any of these guys I've gotten fond of to end up like Jed and the other kid. But wanting to be part of the group, I send those thoughts away and open another beer.

The cool night air seeps into my skin, but each beer warms my insides a little more. The voices around me become louder the more we drink. I start to feel part of the gang as I listen and laugh when each guy tells their story of the team's exploits on the field and off. Jerry, our captain says, "Hey, congratulations on your touchdown run in the game tonight."

My head grows just a little and I wonder if Sarah

was at the game and saw my accomplishment.

Later, about midnight, our diminished attention keeps us from noticing the red and blue lights heading toward us, coming down the path to the lake until it's almost too late to escape.

"Run, everyone for themselves!" Jason yells. "Someone must have narced on us."

I jump in Jacob's truck, but the old vehicle sputters and doesn't want to start. The cop cars block the drive, and I end up being the only one left for the police to take in.

~

Jacob's shoulders sag when he enters the police station to get me. His face shows more age than his sixty-plus years. I sit with my head down. There's no sense in trying to explain, and Jacob doesn't ask me to. I feel as if I'll never be forgiven for this. The buzz from the many beers I drank leaves my head exchanged for a feeling of sorrow.

Coach Raimond calls me into his office on Monday morning. "Tom, I know you weren't the
only one of my players out there by the lake. Now is the time to let me know who they were.
You shouldn't have to take the punishment alone."

I sit with my head down, silent.

Coach Raimond waits for another few minutes. "Okay, well, I'm so sorry, Tom. I'm going to have to cut you from the team. The rules about drinking while playing sports are clear cut. No exceptions. You won't be able to play in next week's sectional game."

I sulk in my room for several days. One evening, Jacob knocks. Opening the door, I see the concern on his face and begin to blubber. "I'm so sorry I let you down."

Jacob grabs me in a hug, and I welcome the touch I've been missing for all the years I'd been with the VanVleets.

For the rest of the term, I go to school only to please the Mulders, but I don't socialize. I spend my time helping Jacob after school and studying each evening. My grades improve, putting me close to the top in my class.

Mrs. Sangor, the school counselor, catches Emily and me at church. "You're doing so well in your classes, Tom. I can look into getting you some scholarships if you think you might want to go to college."

I look away unsure.

Emily's eyes widen, filling her face and she stares my way. "Yes, please do. That would help us out so much."

Late in November, Jacob again calls his cousin, Joan, to wish her a Happy Thanksgiving but also to fish for information about Catherine. "So, any more gossip from Indiana?"

Jacob remains silent while the person on the other end talks freely. When he hangs up, he shares what he learned. "Joan says the VanVleets have had lots of problems with the kids they adopted. She said they still haven't found out where the boy went. And they heard Catherine moved to a home for unwed mothers. She ended by adding, people here are wondering who the father could be because she never was allowed to go out."

When I hear this news, I feel as if I could fight a lion with the rage I'm harboring inside by gut. If it's true that Catherine is pregnant, I'm sure it's Gerrit's baby. My only consolation is Catherine's not around the old guy anymore.

Chapter 25

September 1961-March 1962: Catherine

Each day when I wake, the temperature has dropped to a lower point on the thermometer, and the mornings take longer to warm for outdoor work. Fall leaves turn the Michigan landscape into a multi-hued scene against the deep cerulean sky. Late-season vegetables need to be gathered from the garden, and flower beds are being cleaned daily of debris. The girls close to term are excused from this work, and I envy their leisure time.

If only my morning sickness would stop, I would feel normal again. My new roommate, Patty, hears me retching each morning, and she can't hold it down either. We become quite a similar pair. However, one difference separates us. Patty's parents visit often and bring small gifts. I would love to have the same support, just not from the VanVleets.

When Miss Dawson meets with me in early December, I sit next to her on the two chairs facing her large desk. "Do you think your parents will want to make a visit for Christmas?" The wind whistles through the cracks of the old window in the small office while Miss Dawson waits for my answer.

Ignoring the question, I look down. I run my hands across my swelling belly. I whisper, "I wish I could get rid of this thing inside me."

Miss Dawson replies in a soft voice. "God loves that child, Catherine, even if you don't." She clears her throat. "When you're ready, we can discuss whether you want to keep the baby. Many people would love to have a child. If this is the way you feel, try to think of how happy you would make someone else. Maybe that will help you accept the baby."

My shoulders shake as I try to keep my emotions under control. Pulling my sweater
tighter trying to cover my swollen belly, I say, "I don't want to see this baby. I'm afraid it might look like him."

Miss Dawson rubs my back. Her touch begins to quiet the turmoil inside me. "He raped me, not once, but often and my so-called mother let it happen. I don't ever want to go back there." My sniffles turn into sobs, uncontrollable now.

Miss Dawson reaches across the chair and takes me into her arms. She lets the crying continue until I get it all out. "Let me clarify, Catherine. Are you referring to your adoptive father?"

I nod, studying Miss Dawson's face through watery eyes.

"No, we won't let you go back to that house." Miss Dawson grabs a tissue to wipe tears from her own eyes, too.

In early February, I deliver a healthy baby.

According to my wishes, I don't see the baby and the child is adopted by a loving family. I don't want to know if it's a boy or girl. Also, because of the circumstances in Indiana, I stay and work at the group home for a short time. Before long, a family in a nearby church hires me as their nanny and housekeeper.

The Bakker's large, spacious house becomes my home. I have a bedroom of my own next to the two girls' bedrooms. I've never seen such a beautifully decorated space. The four-poster bed swallows me comfortably when I flop down after Mrs. Bakker shows me where I'll be staying. Soft beige walls soothe my aching insides both physically and emotionally. When I investigate more, I find my attached bath is shared with the girls, but I don't mind. I've never experienced such luxury. At least there's a lock on both doors for privacy.

Peeking into the girls' bedroom, I'm met with an array of pink confetti. The pink comforters and matching pink curtains give the room a sleeping-beauty-princess aura. Small white desks on either side of the room hold combs, brushes, perfumes and miniature dolls left there for future playtimes.

Mrs. Bakker enters the girls' bedroom door with laundered clothing to return, so I tiptoe back to my new room and unpack my few belongings.

When Mr. Bakker returns home with the girls, I'm introduced to the two cutest little angels, and I fall in love. The little girls, ages two and four, both sport heads of blond curls and show their cherub smiles when Mrs. Bakker introduces me.

She says, "Catherine will be your new nanny. She'll watch you when I have to go to work." Suddenly shy, the girls hide behind their dad.

Sitting down on the couch, I grab a children's Bible from the coffee table. "This looks interesting. Want to hear a story?"

Both girls walk over with tentative steps and stand by me as I begin to read the familiar story of Daniel in the lion's den. As I read, I feel little bodies snuggling in next to me. When I look up, the Bakker's stand together, smiling at the scene. Yes, I can do this.

~

Miss Dawson calls in early March to say that Alice telephoned the group home. She had asked when they would be able to pick me up to return to Indiana.

Miss Dawson told her, "Catherine chose to give up the baby. After it was born, she ran away, and we have no idea where she went." The lie couldn't be wrong in this case.

Chapter 26

April 1962: Tom

In the spring, my lab partner, Cindy, surprises me by asking me to go to the prom with her. We've talked quite a bit during Chemistry, but I've felt no stirring within toward her. I like Cindy. She's sweet, but I feel I need to make my intentions clear, so I tell her, "I still have feelings for someone else, so if you still want me to go, it has to be as friends."

Cindy's smile fades and she investigates her lab book for several seconds. "It's a deal."

When I tell Emily I've been asked to prom, she makes it a point to get me into town to rent a tux and order flowers. "What's the matter, Tom? You aren't excited about going?"

I admit I'm not looking forward to the evening. "The day would be perfect if only it was the right girl."

~

Some of Jacob's cows had been bred early in the fall by a bull from another farm. The farmer came and turned the bull out in the pasture with the cows, and the plan was for all the cows to get pregnant and calve early in the spring, so they'd keep producing milk. But, the night of the prom, Susie, the ornery cow, intervenes again. No one has told Susie this night is significant, and she shouldn't disrupt it with the birth of her calf.

When Jacob and I go to the barn to do the milking on Saturday morning, Susie has already begun her labor. Jacob attaches a lead rope to Susie's halter. "Let's get Susie in the calving pen. We want to keep her calm and dry as much as possible."

The day is spent checking up on Susie and ensuring all is ready for the calf's birth. When the time comes for me to get cleaned up and dressed for the dance, I procrastinate, waiting until only a half-hour before I need to leave.

Jacob assures me, "You don't need to worry about Susie. I've done this so many times I can do it in my sleep. You go and have a good time."

I arrive several minutes late to pick up Cindy. Her mom makes me feel welcome. "Come in, Tom. We want to take a few pictures before you go on to the high school. I told Emily that I'll get some printed for her, too."

We pose in front of the large fireplace in the living room. Cindy's blue dress compliments my navy tux and blue shirt and tie, all coordinated by Cindy and Emily ahead of time.

"You kids have fun," says Cindy's dad. Her parents stand on the porch to wave as Cindy and I drive off in Jacob's truck. My thoughts drift to another girl and what it would have been like if Sarah had been my date. Would I have had to meet her at the prom so her parents wouldn't know?

The gym has been transformed into a prom venue. Crepe paper streamers hang from the tops of the doorways and the basketball backboards. Bright-colored balloons tied together and mounted wherever the decorating committee could find an open spot serve as more decorations. Card tables with white tablecloths dot the outer edges of the floor, leaving a large open area where some kids are already dancing to the DJ's records. I have never been to a dance before, and my hands begin to sweat thinking about dealing with the whole evening. As we enter the gym, Cindy leads me over to a group of her friends and they welcome me without questions. Sitting and listening to their chatter, my heart rate slows to normal again.

The evening goes well for a while, with me only stepping on Cindy's toes a few times as we slow dance. However, seeing Sarah in the arms of Jason when they dance together makes my insides boil. I remind myself that I'm the one who left Sarah standing, but it doesn't change how I feel.

Winding my way through the crowd to the punch bowl to grab some drinks for Cindy and myself, I ladle out two glasses. Jason moves so near me I can smell his breath. Slurring his words and grabbing my arm to steady himself, he says, "Hope you're okay with me dating your girl. Guess you guys aren't an item anymore, right?"

"Hey, watch out. You almost made me spill."

"Sorry." Jason holds his hands up in self-defense.

"You've been drinking. Make sure you don't drive when it's time to leave." I shake my head and step away to walk back to Cindy, punch glasses in hand, but thoughts of Sarah riding home with that drunken creep fill my head.

The door opens, shedding light from the hall into the dimly lit gym. Jacob strides over to where Cindy and I are sitting, talking to her friends. Breathing hard and gulping in breaths between his words, Jacob says, "Tom, I'm so sorry, but I need you to come back to the farm. Susie is having an awful time, and I don't want to lose her. I called Dr. Werner, but he's out of town."

I look at Cindy and stand to go. "So sorry." I make sure Cindy's friends will take her home and rush into the cool night air with Jacob.

"Wait." It's Sarah's voice. I haven't been around her often lately, but I'll always recognize the sound of her voice. "I heard Jacob. I can help. I've helped Dad with birthing calves ever since I was little. Besides, Jason's drunk, and I don't want to go home with him."

Jacob takes off in Emily's car, and Sarah and I run to the pickup to follow. I've never seen Jacob drive this fast, and as I try to keep up, small papers fly from the dash out the open window into the chilly spring evening. After a bit, I roll up the glass and glance at Sarah. Her pale-yellow prom dress looks great with her blond hair. I want to tell her how beautiful she looks, but she's staring out the passenger window like a statue. How can I blame her? I was the one who left her standing.

Emily runs from the barn to meet the group when we pull up. "She's about the same." She looks at Sarah. "Let's get you something else to put on. We don't want you to ruin your dress."

Minutes later, Sarah rushes into the barn dressed in old jeans, one of my shirts, and old rubber boots, followed several steps behind by Emily. I've shed my jacket and tie and covered my clothes with a pair of coveralls Jacob always leaves hanging in the barn.

Jacob explains to Sarah, "Susie's labor hasn't progressed like it should. It's been going on much longer than usual."

Sarah prepares to examine Susie and dons a rubber glove to push her hand into the cow.

After a few seconds, she says, "The calf has its legs underneath like it's laying down. So, I'll have to push the calf back and work the legs up one at a time."

While Sarah works, Susie lets out several loud bellows, her contractions working against what Sarah is trying to accomplish. I hold Susie as still as possible while Jacob makes sure Susie doesn't step back onto Sarah. Once Sarah turns the calf to come front feet first, she removes her arm. The water bag appears soon after, followed only a few minutes later by the baby calf. After the birth, the calf lies in the clean straw shaking its head and begins to snort to clear its airways.

Jacob gives Sarah a hug. "That was literally a life saver. Thank you for coming, Sarah."

Sarah laughs and looks toward me. "It was a good excuse to get away from a bad situation."

Once the danger passes and Susie expels the afterbirth, Sarah and I walk out into the still night together.

"That was amazing what you did. Thank you. I know Jacob needs every one of those cows. Losing Susie would have been a huge loss."

Sarah nods and looks up, smiling my way.

That smile goes right into my heart, and I reach for her waist. "Sarah, I don't care if your parents don't like me. We belong together. Look at how well we worked together tonight."

Sarah's arms envelop my neck. "I know." Our lips find each other's, and we kiss like we've never been apart.

Chapter 27

July 1962: Tom

When I come home mid-summer and say I enlisted in the service, Emily bursts into tears. She walks to the shelf to stare at her son's military photo. "Tom, you're supposed to go to college. We've worked hard getting you signed up and applying for scholarships."

"I'm sorry. This recruiter in town made it sound like a good deal, and the poster behind him on the wall makes it look exciting. I'll probably get drafted before long anyway."

Emily wipes her eyes with her hanky, her voice shaky. "Not if you went to college like we planned."

My heart nearly breaks to see Emily's reaction. I didn't want to hurt either of the Mulders. Going into the service is supposed to relieve their burden of paying for college. This will be a good decision in the long run. It's not that I want to be a hero or anything, in fact my stomach's felt like a miniature lawn mower ever since I signed the papers. What have I done? Thinking of possible active duty makes me shake down to my toes.

Jacob looks up from his seat at the table. "Did you already sign, Tom? Because if you didn't, you don't have to go through with this."

"Yeah, I'm eighteen, so the recruiter said I didn't need anyone to sign for me."

I stand there, twisting my cap around in my hands, waiting for my foster parents to get used to the idea. I'd like to go to college, but I don't want Jacob and Emily to go into debt to send me. The scholarships will help, but the Mulders still would need to pay a large share. I love them too much to let them do that. I don't want them to go into debt again. Besides, the recruiter said I could go to college on the GI Bill later. But, explaining that to the Mulders right now is useless. They've been so excited about me going to college in the fall.

Emily begins busying herself making dinner, and Jacob sits at the kitchen table with his head in his hands. After several minutes, the quiet in the room closes in on me. "Come on, Charlie, let's go for a run."

I open the screen door, and Charlie bounds out. This time I hold onto the door and make sure it doesn't slam. I don't want to frazzle their nerves any more than I have.

When I pick Sarah up that evening for our usual ride around the countryside, I try to act as if nothing has changed, but before long, Sarah lays a hand on my arm. "What gives, Tom? Something's up. You're acting all jittery."

I look at her and smile, "Man, you know me too well now."

I pull into the lane that leads back to the picnic area near the lake. Parking the truck so we have a clear view of the water, its surface shimmering, mirroring the sunset. The late June sky paints a glorious array of oranges, yellows, and blues.

Indifferent to the scene, Sarah asks me again, "Are you gonna spill the beans, Tom? Did you get another scholarship?"

I turn to face Sarah, holding both her hands in mine. "I enlisted in the army."

Sarah tries to pull away, but I hold tighter. "What? No! What about our plans to go to college together?" Sarah's voice rises as she talks. Her clear blue eyes bulge from their sockets filling her small face.

Waiting for her to let this news sink in, I keep rubbing my hands over hers. After a bit, I go on in a soothing voice. "Listen, I love you and want to be with you, but I can't do this to Jacob and Emily. I owe them so much already. If I go to the service, they won't have to pay anything for my schooling." I feel tears form at the corners of my eyes. I plead, "It'll just put our plans back a couple of years. We can do this."

Sarah pulls away, this time managing to slide as far from me as possible in the small truck cab. She begins to sob as she talks. "It's not only that you'll be away, but they might send you into battle, and who knows if you'll make it back or in what shape."

"I promise. I'll come back," is all I can say.

~

The rest of the summer becomes a constant struggle for Sarah and me. When I ask her to go to the church picnic with me, her answer makes me wonder what's going on inside her head.

"I promised my mom I'd go shopping with her that day. She wants to spend time with me before I leave for school."

I kick the rocks below my feet. "I'd sort of like to spend some fun time with you, too, before I leave."

Sarah laughs but I don't appreciate her teasing. "You should have thought of that before you signed up for the service without even checking with me."

The night before Sarah leaves for college, I want to take her out for dinner, but she complains that she's too busy getting everything packed. We say a strained good-bye, but we both promise we'll write as often as we can.

In the fall of '62, my first stay as a U.S. Army private is at Fort Bragg, North Carolina, for basic training. Next, I'm assigned to the 2nd Platoon, Company E, 2nd Battalion, 1st Brigade. From there, I'm transferred to Fort Sill near Lawton, Oklahoma. During the three-month stay at Fort Sill, I learn how to operate a variety of field artillery guns, which I later will utilize in the jungles and mountains of Vietnam.

April 1963
Dear Sarah,
Well. Hi, from Vietnam. I miss you so much. We were flown up to Camp Radcliff at An Khe from Saigon. Our first week was pretty easy. They must have been letting us get used to being here. First, we guarded bridges along Highway 19. Now, we got orders to guard a village at the base of some mountain. We marched till my feet ached and camped along the trenches. The fighting started, but most of us were fine.

That's kind of how things go here. Lots of movement and too much downtime. So, I'm going to be okay. I miss you and love you. Can't wait to get home and hold you in my arms. I haven't heard from you for a while. Maybe it's this darn mail here. Please write as much as you can. Your letters are the only thing that keeps me going.

Love, Tom

~

Vietnam turns out to be quite beautiful, with its white-sand beaches. Further inland, its emerald, green rice paddies, quaint-looking mud and straw huts, locally called hooches, dot the landscape. A background of lush green jungle covers the Mieu Mountains. If I didn't know better, I might be lulled into thinking this was a vacation far from home.

My platoon and I are sent to a small village near the Mieu Mountains. Contact with the enemy is sporadic for the platoon. The VC usually cut and run if the fight isn't to their advantage. But this time, the VC gets caught in their own plan for victory. The village is boxed off by a trench system meant to be full of VC and NVC troops, but only a few remain to protect the village. Huey choppers by the dozen come roaring into the rice paddies and drop six or eight additional men far enough away to be out of small arms range. There's no gunfire from the village until my platoon gets within fifty feet, and then there's only light sniper fire. The platoon sergeant, a lifer, leads the way. As I peek over the edge of the trench, one of the VC gets off a shot, and the sergeant rears back. The bullet creases his forehead and knocks him cold.

"I'm dragging him back," yells my buddy, Paul, a soft-spoken guy from Illinois. I follow. Together we drag the sergeant back, where he soon recovers.

For the remainder of the afternoon, clearing the trenches of enemy troops and moving civilians from the village becomes our platoon's work. The trenches are a haven for my buddies and me. As darkness falls, the fighting dies, and silence falls over the village.

"Don't get too settled," says the sergeant. "You can't trust this quiet."

Paul and I take turns watching out and trying to rest. "Hey, thanks for backing me up earlier. I don't think I could have pulled him back alone."

I snicker. "Yeah, that went against everything I've been telling my girl. I've been promising her I won't try any heroics, but she doesn't know what it's like here."

Early in the morning, two of my fellow trench-mates begin shooting at what appears to be a lone figure crawling from a hooch. The figure falls, and at first light, we find a young villager, only about eighteen, with an American M-16 strapped across his back. Would I have shot him if I could? There's no doubt in my mind that my buddies did the right thing, but nothing in this war makes any sense.

Sweeping through the village that morning, there's heavy resistance at first, but as the day wears on, only the job of mopping up remains. The multi-day operation is considered a huge victory.

The war continues, and I count the days until I can return home to Sarah. Every day at mail call, my hopes plummet when no letters arrive.

On the march again in early June of '63, the light green sea of waist-high elephant grass looks inviting, but its serrated edges slice our bear arms. The long blades also give up dry leeches, which stick to exposed skin like little vampires. The day drags on for the whole platoon knowing base camp is on the other side of the ridge.

There's a disturbance in the grass. Everyone's on alert. Because of the height of the grass, I can't tell what it is. What I can see is that it's coming right toward us. When it gets to about ten feet away, I can see, it's one pissed-off-looking wart hog in a path moving directly toward me. I make sure no one is in my line of fire and pull off several rounds.

"Great work, private," yells my sergeant from up ahead, but we keep marching.

~

When there's down time here, I think about Catherine, wondering what's happening with her. Having Sarah in my life makes me want to reconnect with my sister more. I would love to have Sarah and Catherine meet. In my next letter to Jacob, I ask him if he would contact his cousin Joan again and try to find out more about my sister.

Chapter 28

September 1963: Rev. DeJong

After several phone calls from a guy named Jacob Mulder from Nebraska, Rev. DeJong makes up his mind to call on Gerrit VanVleet, the old guy, Jacob is so determined for him to check on. Jacob is somehow connected with VanVleet's son, who is now in Viet Nam. Mulder asks if DeJong could find out where Catherine VanVleet is living so he could pass the information on to the brother, Tom. DeJong was in the service himself, so anything he can do to make a soldier's life better, he's willing to do.

When Rev. DeJong pulls into the driveway, the quiet on the farm unnerves him, and he slams the car door as he gets out, to let Gerrit know someone is there.

The barn looks as if it could fall down any moment. An old rusty tractor sits next to a dilapidated tool shed, and the house has weathered to somewhere between brown and greyish black. Walking up the overgrown sidewalk, he's careful not to stumble on several spots of upheaved cement. The steps to the house feel as if they won't hold his two hundred pounds, so he grabs the porch post in case and carefully makes it across the spongy wood of the porch to knock.

VanVleet comes to the door after several more tries of loud knocking, opens the inner door, and peers through the screen door at the pastor. His greasy hair sticks out from under a cap, and he's wearing a dirty flannel shirt, smelling like soap and water have not touched him for weeks.

"What do you want?" is his greeting.

Rev. DeJong holds the heavy wooden outer door open with his leg. It feels ready to fall from its hinges. "Haven't seen you in church for months. Wanted to see how you're doing."

"Haven't been feeling all that good." To DeJong's surprise, VanVleet opens the screen door to let him in.

When they enter the dark living room, the musty smell penetrates the pastor's nostrils, and it's all DeJong can do to keep from grabbing his hanky from his pocket. Gerrit motions for him to sit, so he moves to a sagging, worn couch, with areas of padding showing through the fabric.

The two spend some time talking about the weather, how the church is doing and whether Gerrit needs any help with the farm. Rev. DeJong asks, "Have you heard anything from either of your kids? If you'd reach out to them, I bet they'd visit and maybe be willing to come back and help."

Gerrit harrumphs. He stares toward the kitchen before answering. "It didn't work out with those two like Alice and I expected. Guess the good Lord knew we weren't cut out to be parents." He removes his cap and rubs his head, pulling his long hair back again to put the cap back on. "I don't know where either is. Sure, would like to, though."

DeJong sees the chance he had prayed for. "I could maybe help. I've got a few contacts all around the Midwest. Do you have any idea where they were when you last heard?"

Gerrit sits back in his chair and studies the preacher. The silence stretches into long minutes. Is he suspicious of his motives? DeJong keeps his face blank, trying to give nothing away.

Gerrit clears his throat, looking down at the floor. "Alice and I took Catherine to a place in Michigan when she got into trouble." He stops and looks up at the pastor. "If you know what I mean. Later we heard she ran off from there after she had the baby. She always was a handful."

"Well, that's something. If you can remember the name of the place, I might be able to do some checking for you. I grew up in Michigan," says DeJong, trying not to sound too anxious.

Gerrit hesitates. He pushes himself from his chair with bones creaking and walks into the hallway leading to the bedroom. DeJong has trouble breathing. He begins to feel a little lightheaded. He can't sit in this suffocating air much longer. Has VanVleet fallen asleep back there? He's taking forever. Rev. DeJong thinks of leaving, but just then Gerrit comes shuffling back.

"Here's the name of the place. If you find her, don't believe anything she says about us. I hope she's grown up enough to realize she had it pretty good here."

DeJong stands and heads toward the door, taking the paper from Gerrit's hand, wanting to get back out and breathe some fresh air. "This is great. I'll let you know if I come up with anything. Hey, looking forward to seeing you in church again soon."

"Yeah, maybe." Gerrit closes the door behind DeJong with a scraping of the ill-fitting screen door. DeJong walks back to his car as if heading to a fire, needing to get to dinner and a council meeting. Calling Jacob will have to wait until he gets home from that.

~

The phone rings just as Jacob gets up to go to bed. Rev. DeJong begins talking as soon as Jacob says hello. "I apologize for the late hour, but our council meeting lasted longer than usual. I know you and Emily will want the information I found out, so I decided to call anyway."

Becoming wide awake, Jacob says, "Yes, it's fine, go on."

"It was a difficult meeting, and Gerrit is a hard guy to talk with, but I presented this as if he might want to contact his kids so they can help him with the farm work. He's not well and can't keep up the farm on his own much longer. He's deluded himself into thinking they might want to come back. So, he gave me the name of the facility where they took Catherine. Unfortunately, I don't have a phone number."

Jacob grabs a pencil and writes the name of the home located in mid-Michigan. DeJong goes on, "I think Gerrit finally decided to cooperate because I let him think I have some contacts, which I do, and I promised to try to find out where his kids are now. It wasn't a lie, so I don't feel bad about this. Maybe there's hope for forgiveness between the father and the kids."

Jacob knows that's not going to happen, at least not on Tom's part, but he doesn't say that to Rev. DeJong. Instead, he assures the pastor the information he has passed on is the right thing to do.

The next day, Jacob begins making calls to different phone operators around Michigan where DeJong indicated the home to be located, trying to find the number of the facility. Finally, after twenty minutes of searching, one helpful operator finds the number. With trembling fingers, Jacob dials the number of Birthright Fellowship.

At first, the care home director won't divulge any information, especially over the phone, but Jacob isn't ready to give up. In a letter, he pleads his case in depth. He explains to Director Dawson that Catherine's brother is in Vietnam, and Jacob wants to find his sister so Tom can reconnect when he's discharged.

Another week passes. The director breaks protocol and calls Jacob. "I've been in contact with Catherine and received permission from her to give you her address and phone number, so you can pass it on to her brother."

"This is great. I can't thank you enough."

The director goes on. "Because of the situation in Indiana, the staff felt Catherine should not return there. So instead, we helped her reestablish herself in a small town in Michigan. She opted to give up her baby for adoption because she didn't want to be reminded of her adopted father every time she looked at the baby."

"Such a sad situation. I'm sure you did the right thing. My wife and I will add your work into our prayers."

Jacob writes all this information to Tom in his next

letter. All those weeks of investigation have paid off, and Jacob can hardly wait to hear Tom's reaction.

Chapter 29

October 1963: Tom

The night we return to Base Camp I receive a letter during mail call, but it's not the message I've been waiting for.

Oct. 24, 1963

Dear Tom,

I'm sorry I haven't written. I know you look forward to my letters. The truth is, and there's no other way to say this. I've met someone at school that I like. We have some of the same classes, and things just happened. We're dating steadily. I feel awful letting you know this way, but I don't want you to keep hoping for a future together.

Please forgive me.

Sarah

After that letter, I don't care how many risks I take, and I seldom worry about mail call now. Without Sarah's letters to look forward to, it's not worth checking.

As the months continue, my combat troop spends

much of our time patrolling the countryside searching for Viet Cong guerilla fighters or North Vietnamese Army forces. We've finished moving through the rural villages near our Base Camp encountering only small skirmishes.

Back at camp, sitting around a small campfire, Paul, one of my good buddies, reads from a newspaper issued to soldiers. "Says here the monks are protesting the government's raids on Buddhist pagodas." He shows everyone some photos of Buddhist monks setting themselves on fire. He reads on, "Also says the government of South Vietnam is on the verge of collapse. Man, makes me wonder if this country's worth fighting for."

Another one of the guys says, "What are we doing here, anyway? If they can't get along among themselves, how are we supposed to tell who's the enemy?"

More grumbles and comments come from other guys. There's nothing for me at home, so I don't add much. I don't want to worry about the dynamics here in Vietnam. I'm just doing what I'm ordered to do, biding my time.

Our platoon leader walks up carrying a bundle of letters and drops them in my lap. "Hey, quit ignoring mail call, will ya?"

I look at the handwriting. All the letters are from either Jacob or Emily. I leave the group to sit alone on my cot to read the letters. Most are from Emily. She must be making it her job to try to keep me from getting depressed. I smile to myself, remembering her sweet face.

After Sarah's letter, I wrote to Jacob and Emily

about her breaking up with me. I felt they needed to know. Besides, I didn't want them writing news to me about Sarah.

As I open each letter from Emily in sequence, the news of home makes me long to see the Nebraska farm again and romp to the creek with Charlie. Emily shares the news about all our church friends, but never once mentions Sarah. She always closes with an uplifting Bible verse and in one envelope, she included a photo of Charlie. I begin reading Jacob's letters. The first couple relay crop prices and the outlook for rain, boring stuff, but he means well. Then I read Jacob's most recent letter, and this news brightens my outlook immediately.

Jacob tells in the letter how he's been working to find out as much as possible about my sister, Catherine. He's been in contact with his cousin, Joan, in Indiana many times since I left, and the puzzle pieces are starting to fall into place. Joan put him in touch with the VanVleet's new pastor, Rev. DeJong. DeJong told Jacob that my adopted mother, Alice, recently passed away from a heart attack. I stop reading for a moment, assessing my feelings. When no sadness surfaces, I read on.

The letter continues by saying Rev. DeJong hadn't been talking to Gerrit because he hasn't been to church lately. However, after several more calls, Jacob convinced him to make a visit to VanVleet to press him on where they took Catherine. Getting to the point, Jacob writes, we've found Catherine followed by several exclamation marks. At the bottom of the paper is Catherine's address. Jacob promises to tell me more details when I get back home.

I stare at the address for several minutes wondering if Catherine will want to hear from me. Will she have forgiven me for leaving her with VanVleet? It's worth a try. My fingers shake as I take a paper from my duffle bag and begin writing.

Chapter 30

January-April 1964: Tom

January 1964

Dear Catherine,

I don't quite know how to start. I'm in Vietnam, but my year here is about over. I'll be flying into Chicago at the end of April. I only have a couple more months to stay out of gunfire. It's been quite an experience, and maybe I'll volunteer for another tour. But first, I want to see you and see if I can get you to forgive me. I'll land in Oakland, process out, and fly from San Francisco to Chicago. Would you be willing to meet me in Northwest Indiana to talk?

After leaving that fateful night from the VanVleets, I ended up in eastern Nebraska with the best people you'll ever meet. And I do hope you will be able to meet them sometime. Their names are Jacob and Emily Mulder. Yes, they're Dutch, but nothing like Gerrit and Alice. I didn't mean to stay as long as I did with them, but Jacob found out you weren't with the VanVleets anymore, and they were so kind to me. So, it ended up being a good choice.

I never should have left without you that night. Please forgive me, Catherine. I need to see you face to face, so I know you understand. Please write back and say you'll meet me.

With all my love, Tom

It's agony waiting for a letter from Catherine, but it finally arrives, and she agrees to meet me. At least now I have something to look forward to during the rest of my tour.

In late March, when my buddies and I leave Vietnam on a plane loaded for the states, the cheering explodes along with the feeling of being lifted off the ground. More wild applause follows when the plane lands in San Francisco. But when we walk through the airport, most travelers show complete indifference or make snide remarks, looking with nasty faces at us troops instead of applauding us.

I would love to scream at those in the airport who act so self-righteous, knowing some soldiers have given the ultimate sacrifice and left chunks of their young and healthy bodies behind for the good of our country. But instead, I try to wear a smile on my face and concentrate on my future meeting with Catherine, only a few more weeks away.

The bus ride from the airport in Chicago to NW Indiana lasts longer than I planned, the bus making many more stops than I had expected. At first, I'm too excited to sleep, but as the trip drones on, I doze between stops. After a couple hours of travel, finally pulling into the parking lot of the Howard Johnson's, I scan the area for Catherine, hoping she hasn't given up waiting for me. Carrying my heavy duffle bag, I disembark and walk toward the restaurant. My first instinct is to run and grab her in a huge hug when I spot her sitting on the bench behind the bus. But I stop to think over the situation. What if Catherine's still upset with me? Maybe she only came because she's angry with me and wants to set things straight.

As I stand there, Catherine turns. Her face breaks into a huge smile. She looks great. A printed headband holds back her long dark hair, and a worn sweater covers a plain white blouse. She stands, hikes up her too-large jeans and runs into my arms. We hug, and I can feel her body begin to shake with sobs. I bite my cheek to hold back my own tears. We pull apart to look at one another, and laughter replaces the sobs and tears.

"Tom, you've grown much taller, and I can feel those muscles under your shirt." Catherine walks around me to check me out better. "I'm so proud of you. I heard from Jacob that you received a Distinguished Service Cross after rescuing guys in your platoon."

Relieved, I stand a little straighter. "You talked to Jacob and Emily?" I ask, ignoring the reference to my heroism. "What do you think of them?"

"Yes, I enjoyed getting to know them, a little." She touches my arm. "I can understand why you stayed with them."

Because she's so understanding, my emotions get the best of me. I can't hold it in any longer. I fold inward, ashamed for Catherine to see my weakness, but she takes me into another hug, and we stand together, oblivious to the onlookers, until the tears subside.

"Let's go get some coffee," says Catherine, and arm

in arm, we make our way into the restaurant.

Catherine questions me about my life with the Mulders, and I share some of the funny stories from my life on the farm and I brag about my dog, Charlie. Wanting to keep things on a happy note, at least for a while, I don't mention Sarah. When Catherine asks about my experiences in Vietnam, I answer, "I met some great guys. They helped me get through my tour. Now I'll be able to go to college on the GI Bill. I've decided not to volunteer for more service."

Catherine's face lights up. "I'm glad to hear that."

Silence follows as the waitress asks if she can get us more coffee, which we both accept. However, we're not finished with what needs to be said, so, after the waitress leaves, I begin again, "Catherine, like I said in my letter, I feel like I made the biggest mistake of my life by leaving you there that night. I hope you can forgive me."

Catherine's eyes tear up, and she swipes at the corners. "There's nothing to forgive. None of it was your fault." Staring out the restaurant window, she continues, "It was hard, but looking back, things have turned out okay, and now I'm working for my church and taking college classes and taking care of two awesome little girls. It's made me realize I want to be a teacher. I want to work with kids."

"Good for you." I reach across the table for Catherine's hand. "But how was it, with the VanVleets after I left? I need to know, Catherine, and you need to let me bear the burden with you."

Catherine pulls her hand away and pushes her hair away from her face as if clearing out the past. She starts out with a quavering voice. "At first, it was him staring at me all the time, so I tried to stay close to Alice. After you were gone and he healed up, Gerrit would get upset faster, and the beatings were for any little thing he saw fit to reprimand me about. No one noticed at church or school because they made me cover the bruises. After the church picnic, when I stepped over his bounds and entered the games with one of the guys from school, it was like it triggered something in Gerrit, like he was jealous. That night he came to my room and intended to use his belt on me, but his pants fell when he pulled out his belt, which started it all."

Catherine stops, red-faced, and looks away. With a soft, muffled voice, she says, "He forced himself on me, and every time he asked Alice to do the milking because he didn't feel well, I could expect the same."

My temperature rises, and my voice lowers to a growl. "That pervert. He needs to be punished. How could Alice let that happen? At least she's not around anymore to help him. She died not too long ago."

Catherine lifts her head. "Didn't know that, but I don't feel any sadness about it. She was as much to blame."

I slap my palm on the table and make the cups jump. "I never should have left you. I'll have to live with this the rest of my life."

"I didn't tell you so you could dwell on it, and I don't want to talk about it again. Go back to Nebraska and make a life. Go to college and find a nice girl to marry. The important thing is that I got away from them. When I got pregnant, Gerrit tried to make Alice believe it wasn't his. She arranged for me to go to an unwed girls' home, and after that, the people there helped me find work, so I didn't have to return to that evil place. I regret giving up the baby, but I knew I couldn't look at it or love it if it looked like Gerrit."

"I'm sure the baby has a great home. Not like the VanVleets," I say, reaching across and squeezing Catherine's hand.

The restaurant starts filling for the lunch hour, and I pay for our coffee. We move out into the bright sunshine, reluctant to separate. "What now?" I ask. "Going back to Michigan right away?"

"Probably. But I might do a little sightseeing before going back. The Bakkers let me use their extra car whenever I need it. So, I may as well take advantage of it. Driving with the window cracked a bit to let in the spring air makes me feel like I'm free to do whatever I want. What about you?"

"I'm catching another bus to Nebraska. I've got to see Jacob and Emily before I do anything else. I'm anxious to see my dog, Charlie, and help out on the farm again. I'll get Emily to help me sign up for college in the fall. She loves to do things like that."

We embrace and promise to write and get together again soon. I don't let on what's lingering in the back of my mind.

Chapter 31

April 1964: Catherine

Driving the Bakker's small compact into the gas station next to the Howard Johnson's, I pull up to the pump. The tinted windows keep me from seeing inside the bus to catch a last glimpse of Tom. As the attendant fills the car with fuel, I wonder when Tom and I will be able to visit again. Maybe I can go to see him in Nebraska. The Mulders would be wonderful to get to know, so opposite from Gerrit and Alice.

It was everything I could do to keep my anger under control while discussing those degenerates with Tom. Telling him about my experience only made me more determined. My story was a sugarcoating of the truth. My life became a nightmare after Tom left that night, but I didn't want him to feel responsible. I couldn't tell him what I plan to do to get back at Gerrit for that awful treatment. He would either try to stop me or insist on going along. Neither one is an option.

From the day I received Tom's letter wanting to meet in Indiana, thoughts of what I would do there kept repeating in my head. I would use the visit with Tom as an excuse to borrow my employer's car and add a few extra miles on it after our meeting to return to the VanVleets. The Bakkers told me to enjoy myself, and this is the best fun I can think of. Remembering that first night alone with Gerrit and the other episodes afterward makes my insides churn with mounting revenge. Ever since the birth of the baby, sleep often eludes me while my thoughts run rampant, planning how I'll make Gerrit suffer.

I remember those beady squinty eyes the most. My nightmares always include him coming toward me and staring at me with those piercing eyes. Stopping that stare by wrapping my scarf around his head and tying his hands so he can't get it off will be the best possible payback. Maybe I should leave him stumbling around in that dilapidated old house, unable to see where he's going. But, no, I won't stop there. Tying his feet so he can't walk will be sweet justice. See how he likes that. But the best part will be having him wonder what I'm up to while I get ready to leave and leave him tied there. These thoughts make me queasy, and sweat pours from my forehead, but imagining these schemes makes me feel somewhat avenged.

I pay for the gas and thank the attendant for cleaning my windshield with an extra dollar for a tip. In case Tom is looking, I wave as I pull back onto the road heading south, humming along with the radio.

Before long, the busy road changes to country driving. The scenery shifts from businesses lining the side of the road to new green growth on the trees, grass fringes, and freshly plowed fields waiting for planting.

While driving along the back roads, the window

cracked to enjoy the fresh, cool air and the radio blaring, my face breaks into a smile. The bright spring day makes for a lovely drive into the country, and I try not to compare it with the first time I followed this road. For Tom and me, the road south led to a life of fear and punishment. I can't forgive the people of the small town either. They should have investigated, but no one wanted to make waves. When I got pregnant, someone should have guessed and confronted the VanVleets, but instead, Gerrit and Alice hushed it up and let everyone think I had been seeing a young man. If only that had been the case.

The car begins to shake unexpectedly, breaking into my thoughts, and I have quite the time hanging onto the steering wheel. Slowing the car down to a crawl, the bumping only becomes worse. I get out to investigate after pulling off the road when I find a field driveway. The deflated rear tire on the driver's side needs immediate fixing. This can't be happening, but I'll have to deal with it. I've never changed a tire before. However, I've watched others do it, so I open the trunk and start getting out the jack and other tools I need.

A noisy pickup pulls to a stop near the Bakker's car. "Looks like you may need a little help," the middle-aged guy says through his open window.

He looks harmless, but I am wary of any man, so I say, "No, I can handle it. Thanks anyway."

"Suit yourself."

After he drives away and I have trouble loosening one of the lug bolts, I wish he would return. With a super-human shove to the lug wrench, the bolt gives, and I fall on my knees. Catching myself against the car, it leans precariously. Why was I so stubborn about accepting help? With the care of a surgeon, I finish the repair and pray the tire will hold until I can stop at a service station to have someone check it out.

When I drive through my former town, few memories touch me, having never been allowed to interact with the local teenagers. The grocery store where Alice and I bought a few items every Saturday still looks open, although needing a coat of paint and cleaning up, like all the stores on Main Street. With only the time it takes to wink, I'm already driving out of town.

Stopping at the Shell Station on the outskirts, I wait another fifteen minutes for the service attendant to check out my work. By this time, my insides feel like shooting stars, all heading in opposite directions along with my courage. I dredge up the memory of Gerrit's advance and my resolve again swells like a rushing current.

With the mechanic's approval, I drive south toward the fateful location of the VanVleet farm. As I draw closer, fear grips my insides. Old Gerrit can't compete with my youth, but what if someone stops by and sees what I'm doing and calls the police? Jail is not an option, not when my life is beginning to come around. I'll have to be careful not to cause attention.

Turning down the county road that leads to the farm, I can see the buildings in the distance. I reduce the car's speed to close to zero, creeping toward my destination. The driveway appears on my left, and I edge the car's front about five feet into the lane. Shutting down the ignition, silence surrounds me. I sit staring at the awful place that holds such chilling memories. The roof has deteriorated more, and the porch looks as if it will fall from the house before long. Everything about the place looks dark and dingy, reminding me of the scary movies I've seen. My eyes are drawn to the upstairs window, the room where it all began, and I push myself to follow through with my plan. Before leaving the car, I don the pair of leather gloves I brought so I won't leave any sign of being here.

Walking toward the house, I pick my way through tall weeds, so my footprints won't be found. Various tools are left in the spot where they were last used. A push mower sits as a monument to a better time at the base of the porch.

Without knocking, I open the front door and enter the house. No one answers when I call out, so I continue searching. The same eerie quiet follows me as I amble from room to room. Sweat forms on my brow regardless of the chill inside the old house and my knees feel as if they might give out, but I push myself to go on.

Entering the couple's bedroom. I can't help but wonder if Alice ever experienced any kind of mutual familiarity inside these walls. A paper on the table beside the bed catches my eye—a funeral announcement for Alice. I feel nothing. Tom had said Alice died, but this makes it real. Only one of them to deal with now.

My feet propel me up the stairway. There's no reason to return to my old room, but I'm drawn to it for some reason. Dizziness overcomes me when I enter the doorway into the bedroom, and I grab the bedpost to keep from falling into that horrible bed. Waiting for clarity, I turn and hurry back down the stairs.

Chapter 32

April,1964: Tom

As the bus sits idling, waiting for all the passengers to enter, the afternoon sun shining through the bus windows keeps me from finding Catherine's car for several minutes. I spot her and watch as she heads out of the restaurant's parking lot into the gas station lot. Satisfied that she'll soon be on her way, I sit back in the comfortable bus seat to try to relax. But as if drawn to Catherine, I lean forward again and check where she is one more time. She pulls out from the gas station and heads south. Odd. She should be traveling north, back to Michigan, although she did say she wanted to do some sightseeing. I sit back again and try not to worry about my older sister.

Knowing the story behind Catherine's time with the VanVleets after I left makes my anger resurface, and my head begins to pound. Though Catherine acts like she's doing well, I can't forgive myself for what she endured those months after I left. What sick person could do that to a young girl? The trip home will be taking me right past Stockwell where I grew up at the VanVleet place. Maybe I should stop there and let the old guy have it.

The closer I get to my former home in Indiana, the more I'm compelled to stop. Letting Gerrit know how well I did in the army after I left them and maybe a little of the same medicine he gave us will complete my revenge. The bus schedule shows a stop at the town ten miles south of my former town, but it wouldn't be the first time I've hitchhiked and walked several miles. And this time, I'll have on my army fatigues to attract rides.

I carry my duffle bag to the front of the bus and begin talking with the driver. I find out the guy's brother has been in Vietnam, so it's easy to converse.

"Bet you're glad to be going home, huh?" asks the driver. "My brother couldn't wait to get out of there. He's had a few issues since he's been home. Can't hold a job and has a drinking problem."

"Yeah, some guys can't put it behind them. I've got some great parents who'll help me adjust." I lean forward in the front seat as if wanting to discuss a pressing issue with the driver. "In fact, when I was little, we lived somewhere around here before we moved to Nebraska. I've been thinking I'd like to go check it out and see if I can find the old place. Could you let me off right around here?"

The driver shoots me a quick glance, sizing me up. "Not supposed to do that. Company policy, you know. But I guess I can do it for one of our brave servicemen." He checks his rearview mirror. "No cars behind me. How's about right now?" He begins to slow the bus down and pulls to a stop on the road.

Thanking the driver, I climb down the steps and wave as the bus pulls away. Nothing looks familiar. I'm not sure how far away the town is from where I'm standing, so I start walking. After about ten minutes, the sound of a car's engine carries through the springtime air from behind me. I turn so the driver can see my uniform and extend my arm and thumb. The car whizzes past, but the brake lights appear. The driver moves the car into reverse and backs up until even with where I stand along the side of the road. A young girl reaches over and rolls down the passenger side window. "I'm only going as far as Stockwell, but I can get you that far."

I open the car door and bend down to peek in at the girl. She's young, a teenager with red hair pulled back into a ponytail. Bright lipstick covers her lips, and a brighter shade adorns her nails. "Thanks. Nice car." Tossing my duffle bag in the back, I settle myself in the passenger seat next to her. She stomps on the accelerator as soon as I do, and we're off.

"It was my graduation present. My mom and dad still haven't gotten over losing my brother, so they spoil me rotten. Car accident," the girl says, smacking her gum to the music. "Vietnam?"

"Yeah." I don't want questions, so I ask, "Your name wouldn't be Thomas, would it?" An image surfaces in my mind of a dark, cold night and a young man begging me to stay with him while he breathed his last. I owe my escape from Stockwell partly to Jed Thomas.

"How'd you know? I'm getting a little freaked out." She slows the car, maybe wanting me to get out.

"The story sounds familiar. Everyone around here

remembers that accident. You had to be a sister to one of those guys. I guessed the right one. I'm from the rival town, Deaver. That was quite the talk for a long time, how Deaver beat Stockwell in the sectional and that awful accident after the game." The small lie of where I am from seems appropriate now.

This must satisfy her because she pushes the car back to speed again. She glances at me and catches me staring at the speedometer. "I know I shouldn't drive fast, what with what happened to my brother, but there's no traffic and dry pavement. What can happen, right?"

"I guess so." I lean back in the seat and try to enjoy the next few miles. The welcome sign for Stockwell looms in the distance, and to her credit, she slows to the speed limit when we enter the town. She pulls into the grocery store's parking lot, indicating this is as far as she'll take me.

"Thanks for the lift. Hey, stay safe." She gives me a thumbs-up, and I climb out and pull my duffle bag from the back. The car begins moving as I'm shutting the door.

A dust cloud hangs in the air, and I start walking to get clear of the haze in the direction of the VanVleet farm. It's only a mile or so out of town, so I don't try for another ride. Coming to the farm on foot may be a better option, anyway. Surprising old Gerrit might work to my advantage. I'm not sure what I expect to transpire when I get there, but I'll figure it out. Ever since I heard how Catherine was treated by Gerrit, my hatred for the couple has reappeared. The more I think about what happened to her, the more I want to do something. Somehow, I need to keep my anger in check and still teach old Gerrit a lesson.

The farm comes into sight, and I quicken my pace. I've got to complete this stopover and return to the bus route soon, so Jacob and Emily won't become too concerned. That means I'll need to take care of business and get back on the road before anyone knows I'm here.

The farm's unnatural quiet makes me slow down as I walk up the lane toward the house, if you can call it that, more like a shack now. There must be even less cash available to repair the steps. The push mower beside the porch reminds me of the punishment I received for not cleaning it properly. My insides begin to boil from that one memory, but the military has taught me how to keep my emotions in check. Walking up the steps, I knock, but no one answers, so I enter the squalid house.

"Anybody home?" The stillness is like a suffocating blanket, my breathing and my steps making the only sounds. As I walk from room to room, memories invade. Stopping the pain and bitterness becomes impossible. I break out in a sweat, and my heartbeat quickens. I can't stay in here any longer. I run from the house and out into the fresh air.

Gerrit must be in the barn. Can I face him without losing control? Seeing the old guy again will dig up memories I have tried to forget. Best try to focus on the present and memories of the farm in Nebraska. I concentrate on a vision of Jacob's well-kept barn and my foster father's love as I walk the path to the barn before me, full of so many awful memories.

The old Ford pickup and the Chevy sedan rest in the driveway, like lifeless metal sculptures. No tracks extend from their tires. I stagger toward the barn door, expecting to see Gerrit cleaning stalls, but instead, a loud moaning reaches my ears. Stepping up my pace, I move into the interior space of the barn and come to a sudden stop. Gerrit sits on the cement floor, propped up against the same pole where he tied me years ago. Visions of that night bombard my brain.

He's holding a red hanky to his chest. As I move closer, he looks up to see me standing there. "Well, two visitors in one day. How did I get so lucky?"

Not sure what Gerrit is talking about, I don't reply but move in closer. The bloody hanky only covers a small portion of the sticky liquid that is oozing out around the makeshift bandage. Gerrit's soaked coverall is gradually turning red. Pitchfork tines protrude from his chest, the handle extending to the left of the post along the floor as if propping the man into a sitting position.

"What happened to you?" It's obvious, but how did he get in this predicament?

Gerrit's voice quavers with every word, and he stops for a breath between each sentence. "Not that you care. You need to go get some help. I'm going to bleed to death here."

I sit down on a hay bale to think. What if Catherine made it here before me? If Catherine had anything to do with this, getting help right away may be the wrong thing to do. Gerrit will bleed out before a doctor can make it here, anyway, and if I stay, I'll have lots of explaining to do.

"Please, go get some help," Gerrit gasps. More blood squirts from the punctures with each word and breath.

"Like you helped us? I don't think so. See this? The Distinguished Service Cross for Bravery Beyond the Norm. Wanted you to know I turned out fine. No thanks to you and Alice."

Gerrit makes no comment. His head slumps to his chest.

When I leave the farm, I grab a long bundle of straw to wipe away my footsteps on my way out of the barn. I break off a small branch and do the same down the driveway to the blacktop road. No sense letting anyone know I've been here to see Gerrit's last moments.

Chapter 33

April 1964: Tom

I walk away using the same field road I took the night I left several years previous and don't look back. There's no nostalgia, only practicality because it's the shortest route back to the highway. Stopping when passing the bridge where the accident had occurred that night of my escape, I say a prayer for the families of the two boys and the Thomas girl for her safety. Will God answer the prayers of such a sinner like myself?

The familiar highway makes an excellent place to catch a ride to Deaver, where I call the Mulders to give them the time my bus will arrive in the town near our home. I board the next bus heading to Nebraska. Once seated in one of the comfortable bus seats, I lean back and let the last few hours filter through my brain. Assessing the situation becomes an obsession. I can't make myself think of anything else. I had only intended to give Gerrit a once over and let him see how well I had done without their help but seeing Gerrit in that predicament gave me closure, especially after what I learned from Catherine. As far as I'm concerned, Gerrit got what he deserved.

But how had Gerrit ended up in that situation? Could Catherine have made it to the farm before I did and caused the old man to fall on that pitchfork? Whatever or whoever caused it, I'm grateful.

That pastor is the only one who's been there lately. No one else ever stops at that farm. When Catherine and I were small, no visitors ever stopped by. So, it may be days before anyone finds Gerrit. I'll be back home long before that. After several minutes more, my thoughts stop whirring and a partial calm fills my chest.

After closing out those thoughts, I finally doze off to sleep.

~

The bus engine winds down and stops, waking me in the process. I spot Jacob and Emily waiting near a bench in front of the local coffee shop, and my heart swells with devotion. My love for them explodes within me. How had I been so fortunate as to stumble onto their farm back when I was wandering?

Emily is sitting, fidgeting with her dress, and Jacob paces, waiting for the bus door to open. I can't wait to get off the bus to give them hugs. It's been a year and a half since I left for boot camp, and I've not seen them since, only keeping in touch with letters. Lingering impatiently behind others to disembark, I hurry toward the couple after hitting the pavement. Hugs come from Emily, and Jacob shares a handshake and partial hug.

The ride back to the farm becomes a series of questions, and I answer each one as well as I'm able. Emily seems to want things back to how they were, but

I don't know if that can ever happen, not after the things I saw in Vietnam and then just a few hours ago at Gerrit's place.

"Is Charlie, okay?" I ask. "I thought maybe he'd be with you."

Jacob laughs and says, "He's fine. He'll be so excited to see you. We thought it might be too long of a wait for him and for us to control him. That dog sure has been missing you. Every time someone pulls on the yard, he runs out to see them and gets a few pets, but hurries back to his favorite sleeping spot on the porch because it wasn't you."

"Can't wait to see him."

No mention is made of my breakup with Sarah. The mood would be ruined if we did.

Charlie greets the car and barks his welcome all the way up the drive. Does he realize I'm in the car? I bound out of the back seat, and Charlie bounces around me like popcorn sizzling in a pan, finally resting his front paws on my broad shoulders and licking my face.

"Hey buddy, I love you, too, but you need to stay down, now." I lower the dog's paws and lean down to give Charlie the hug he's been craving. "Man, I missed you."

A few days of roaming the farm with Charlie and helping Jacob with the chores helps me calm my fractured nerves, and I begin to feel almost like my old self. Nightmares invade my sleep at times, both of Vietnam and the events back in Indiana with images intertwining in a weird set of circumstances. I dream of the Viet Cong ready to ambush my troop, and then Gerrit's face replaces the oncoming attacker. When I wake, often the bed is drenched. Sometimes I get up and roam outside before going back in to try to get back to sleep.

As the days unfold, the more I concentrate on work, the less the past bothers me, and my life becomes a calmer sea. But this quiet existence may be like waiting for an avalanche to start. Once certain incidents begin shaking the universe, a tumbling of events will follow. Someone will eventually discover VanVleet, and the police will start asking lots of questions. Maybe they'll be able to find out where Catherine and I now live.

~

After several weeks of relearning the farm tasks, my mechanical abilities grow along with the necessity of repairing the older tractors and other equipment Jacob and I buy at farm auctions to save money. Jacob's philosophy tends to be, why buy new when we can get by with fixing the old? I excel at welding after Jacob gives me a few lessons and spend many hours drawing plans in the evening. The drawings come to life when I use the plasma cutter and welder we purchased, great finds from a recently retired neighbor's auction.

My first project is a simple device to tamp down the dirt around new fence posts. Jacob brags. "That works so much better than the hoe handles I used to use."

Another project involves adding a weight to the backside of the two tractor brake pedals, making them flip up independently, so the driver doesn't have to reach down and flip them by hand. Jacob boasts so much about this invention that I keep busy in the shop each evening after chores fabricating the weights for neighboring farmers.

The long workdays on the farm help me to sleep unbothered, and my muscles pop through my shirt from all the chores and farm work.

Catherine and I exchange phone calls weekly, but nothing more is said about the VanVleets. I don't want to be reminded of the past. In fact, I go out of my way to only talk about the things I've been doing on the farm and planning a future visit to Nebraska for Catherine. She doesn't bring them up either.

Chapter 34

May 1964: Rev. DeJong

Missing Gerrit in church again for several Sundays, Rev. DeJong plans to head over to the old man's farm again the following week. He tells himself he should visit more often since Gerrit's been trying to make amends with the congregation. The guy needs some tender care, and DeJong figures his church family are the only ones left in his life who can give it. Those two children sure aren't coming back. Not with the stories DeJong has heard from other parishioners about how they may have been treated. The sad thing is no one did anything about it at the time.

Driving out to VanVleet's farm on Tuesday morning, Rev. DeJong can't help but feel good about this visit. The April mid-morning weather begins with plenty of sunshine to warm the inside of the car, and the radio blasts his favorite hymn station as he moseys along the back roads. He passes the Tuinstra farm, belonging to one of his other church members. The newly painted barn and well-kept farmhouse show

Tuinstra and his family take pride in keeping their place well-tended. The whole family comes to church regularly and gives their tithes without complaint. DeJong says a thank you prayer for people like the Tuinstras, of which many attend his church. Where would he be without them?

Driving further down the road, the VanVleet farm appears in sight. From this range, the difference is noticeable. The building roofs that rise above the tree line need shingling, and the trees could use trimming. Dead trees rise menacingly above the buildings, threatening a significant deluge of branches and limbs if a strong wind picks up.

When Rev. DeJong pulls into the driveway, nothing stirs. No breeze moves the new leaves, popping out on the few live trees. No lights light up the house, and everything looks identical to his previous visit. The tractor sits in precisely the same spot, and neither vehicle has been moved.

DeJong exits his car and slams the door hoping the sound will arouse VanVleet, but no one comes to the door. The minister climbs the rickety stairs and knocks. No answer. He knocks again, much louder this time. Nothing. He steps inside the unlocked door. "VanVleet?" he yells. No answer.

Walking through the house, he calls out VanVleet's name but finds no one. The eerie quiet makes the pastor slow down and walk with reserved steps back out the door and down the path to the barn. Again, he calls, "VanVleet?" several times before walking all the way into the open door of the barn. Before turning the corner into the milking area of the barn, the smell reaches the pastor's nostrils. The distinctive aroma of a body decomposing makes DeJong stop and say a silent prayer. Anyone who encounters this unique smell never forgets it, and Pastor DeJong has had experience with the smell during his tour in Vietnam. It's something you never want to deal with again.

But nothing can prepare DeJong for the sight he encounters when he moves into the next room of the barn. VanVleet's body lays propped against one of the barn's supporting poles, pitchfork tines perforating through where his small chest had been, flesh being eaten by maggots and dried blood covering his clothing. The blood covers a three-foot area where it had trickled away from the body onto the cement of the barn floor. Small animal footprints track through the dried blood, a welcome food ration for the small rodents.

Rev. DeJong knows not to risk contamination of the area, so he moves away from the body the same way he entered, trying to use his same footsteps as he exits the barn. He hurries to his car and drives much faster to the police station than when he came to the farm, needing to report the scene as quickly as possible.

His mind whirls with what he's seen. What happened to Gerrit? Did he trip and fall? That must be the explanation. Feeling guilty, he asks himself why he hadn't come to visit him sooner. At least the body wouldn't be in the shape it's in, and who knows, he may have gotten there in time to call the ambulance and save him. He'll have to live with his neglectfulness, and the gruesome scene etched into his brain. Add it to all the other situations over the years that he'll never be able to forget.

At the police station, Chief Borden calls Rev. DeJong into his office as soon as he enters the station.

Everyone knows DeJong as the minister of the big brick church, and the Chief has had the pastor help before in dealing with touchy situations.

"What's up? You don't look so good." Borden motions DeJong to sit, but he declines and continues to pace.

"You'll have to send a team out to Gerrit VanVleet's place. They might need a few extra people. I was there to check up on him, and he's lying dead in his barn. It's not a pretty sight. Looks like he's been there a while." Unloading and telling someone else about the situation helps the pastor settle his nervous stomach, and he sits in one of the padded chairs across from Chief Borden.

"Okay, Reverend, let's back up. Was anyone else around when you were there? Did it look like foul play or an accident?"

DeJong takes a huge breath and wipes his brow with his hanky. "I don't know. It smells so bad that I didn't want to stick around too long. Thought I better let the pros handle this." DeJong waits for a comment, but the Chief stares, not responding, so he continues. "I was there several weeks ago, but I don't think anyone else has been there beside me for a long time. It looked to me like maybe he fell on his pitchfork. It was sticking right through his chest."

Wide eyes and raised eyebrows fill the Chief's face as he looks back at DeJong from across
the desk. Chief Borden lifts the phone and calls for a team to investigate the VanVleet farm. He tells the person on the other end of the call not to use sirens and lights. "We don't want to call attention to the scene and rouse the local newspaper reporters. We don't need that

yet." He ends the call by saying he'll be there as soon as possible.

"Guess we can take it from here, Rev. DeJong. Go home and try to forget what you saw. I know it's hard to get those images out of your head. Don' beat yourself up. You couldn't have done anything differently."

The clouds have moved in, and with them, cooler temperatures when DeJong leaves the police station. Driving home, he decides to wait to call Jacob Mulder out in Nebraska. The rumors suggest the kid may have had an altercation with VanVleet before leaving years ago, so chances are he won't care about his adopted father's death. The Mulders are doing their best for the kid, so why ruin it? If Chief Borden ever needs to know Tom's whereabouts, that will be the time for DeJong to act.

Chapter 35

May 1964: The Police

The police officers park along the county road across from VanVleet's farm to avoid disturbing any of the scene. Their first item of business is to determine whether this could be a crime scene. The officers who check the deceased will decide if the location should be handled as if foul play might be a possibility.

Officer Manning, the head of the team, walks around the outside perimeter of Gerrit's body. "The way that pitchfork extends through the body looks suspicious. I'm thinking possible homicide."

Manning instructs Officer Jansen to call the county coroner on the car radio and explain the situation. "Tell him to bring someone along who deals with forensics."

While he and the other officers wait for the coroner to arrive, Manning gives directions to his team. "Let's spread out around the barn and house and look for footprints or any other signs of entry."

The officers tramp around the area, adding many footprints but finding no evidence to catalog. The three milk cows, their udders extended beyond normal, stand bawling at the fence. Not milking them for all the days since Gerrit died puts pressure on their udders, and they're now in severe pain. Officer Jansen returns to his police car to call the station and have them send out the town veterinarian.

When the coroner arrives, he and his assistant begin photographing the body at all angles and document everything. They measure the angle of the pitchfork and the length of the blood trails. Samples of insects found on the body are captured, and much time is spent looking for fingerprints they might find in the area and on the pitchfork.

While the coroner works in the barn, probable cause allows the police officers to enter the house. Items left on the counter in the kitchen are documented. They look through the drawers and closets for any additional information and a couple of officers search the vehicles for any evidence of value.

No pieces of torn clothing or signs of struggle are found outside the house and barn. Jansen walks back over to where Officer Manning is standing. "So maybe our initial estimate is correct. Perhaps it's a freak accident."

"I don't know. I still have a feeling we're dealing with something more suspicious."

The coroner's thorough investigation ends with marking the placement of the body and other items related to the death. Gerrit's body is moved with care to be delivered to the morgue, where more tests will be conducted to pinpoint the time of death.

As the officers are wrapping up their work and lifting the body onto the stretcher, the coroner says,

"Everyone hold still." He lifts the pitchfork. "Hey, Manning, does this look like part of a footprint to you?"

Officer Manning returns to the site. "Could be. Guess we missed that. It looks like the edge of a large shoe."

The coroner adds, "When I moved the pitchfork to save it for evidence, I noticed it. No one saw it because the pitchfork handle was covering it."

More photos are snapped. The partial footprint may prove someone had been at the scene.

Chapter 36

May 1964: Tom

The long hours of silence when working alone in the shop make my mind whir with thoughts of my future, the events of the past at the VanVleet farm, and worrying about when or if the police will arrive to question me. Emily insists I apply again for college, and she goes so far as writing for an application, but I love working with my hands and don't feel I'll fit into the college scene anymore.

While showering one morning, the image of Gerrit sitting in the barn bleeding haunts my thoughts, as it does often. I want to ask Catherine if she had anything to do with how I found Gerrit when she calls today for our regular weekly phone call, but I've connected with Catherine again, and I don't want to upset our renewed relationship.

The phone rings after breakfast, and I rush to answer it, hoping it's Catherine, but the woman's voice on the other end is high-pitched and agitated. She asks for Jacob, so I motion for him to come to the phone. I step back to watch as Jacob grabs the phone, primarily listening. Jacob's face soon changes from a smile to a downturned mouth and puckered eyebrows.

After hanging up, he turns to Emily and me, shaking his head. "That was my cousin, Joan, calling from Indiana. Rev. DeJong returned to visit your foster father, and she said he found an awful sight." He looks at me. My unchanged face indicates it's okay to continue. "They found him dead with a pitchfork jabbed through his chest from behind. Guess they think he fell onto it in a freak accident. He was lying in the barn for quite a while, so the body isn't in good shape to tell for sure. She said she would have called sooner but was out of town and just heard the news."

Jacob stares at me again. I look out the window, keeping my face as hard as stone. I make no comment.

Emily says, "Oh, that poor man. Such a freak accident."

I snort, so Jacob asks, "Tom, how do you feel about this? It's got to be a shock even though the man was awful to you and Catherine."

The kitchen becomes as still as a cemetery in winter. A chill settles in the air. Several minutes pass, and the birds outside on the feeder sing their songs and flutter from branch to perch, but my thoughts block out everything except the horror of the past.

"Awful? That's an understatement. He abused my sister many times and got her pregnant," I yell. "He can rot away forever for all we care."

Jacob and Emily freeze in the stances each held before my outburst. I barge out of the house with Charlie in tow. We head for the path to the creek, the place I've grown to love.

Charlie and I don't return until it's time for evening chores, which Jacob and I perform in silence. Later, at dinner, I flop down at the kitchen table, head hung low. After an interminable silence, Jacob asks, "Tom, did you already know about VanVleet?"

Coming back to reality, Emily begins to clean up. "If Tom does know anything about this matter, Jacob, he'll tell us when he's ready." She puts a hand on my shoulder. Her voice raises. "Just my opinion, but I agree with Tom. That man was evil. He isn't worth our forgiveness."

Jacob stares at his wife, then stands to take her in his arms. "What do you think, Tom? Does Emily need to cool it?"

I jump up and give her a hug, too. "She just wants to protect me, her bear cub."

When the dinner dishes are packed up and put away, I go to my room. Thankfully, no one speaks of VanVleet's fate again for weeks.

~

When Charlie needs a trip to the vet for his yearly shots, I load him into Jacob's old truck for his appointment. As the truck ages, two main problems have evolved, romancing the vehicle up to speed which takes forever, and the opposite, coaxing the old truck to stop. At a stop sign along the way, I brake and downshift to stop. Charlie can't help but keep going forward, falling to the floor and jumping back up to sit in the passenger seat again, looking out the window like a regular guy. After several of these episodes, I start stopping about a mile before needed so Charlie can maintain his balance. However, near town, a snazzy red Mustang pulls out around me to pass, meets an oncoming car, whips back in front of my truck and slams on the brakes to avoid hitting the car in front of it. The truck's brakes squeal as I stomp down and try to downshift at the same time. Charlie again falls forward, and this time barfs all over the truck's floor.

"Oh, poor guy, sorry this old truck is giving us such a rough ride. We'll be there soon, and you'll feel better."

But once I pull into the parking lot of the vet's office and open his door, Charlie seems fine and bounces out with excitement. I am left with a mess to clean up. As I grab Charlie's leash and lead him toward the door, I notice the red Mustang parked behind the building. My insides burn, wanting to have it out with the driver, but when we enter the front door, there stands Sarah behind the reception desk, picking up the phone to answer it.

Charlie wags his whole body and pulls at his leash to visit with her. When she hangs up the phone and sees the dog, she emerges from behind the desk. "Hi boy, haven't seen you for a while. You're looking great." Sarah kneels, takes Charlie's face between her hands, and places a kiss on his head.

I stand there, taking in the scene. Her hair is longer and brushed straight, but her bright blue eyes twinkle as before, and her slender figure still entices, filled out more in all the right places. I glance at her left hand; no ring, but there may be a good reason she doesn't wear it here at the vet's office.

Finding my voice, I say, "Still driving like a crazy person, I see. Your wild driving could have killed Charlie and me back there."

"Nice to see you, too." Sarah turns and heads back

to her desk. "What can we do for you?"

"Charlie needs all of his yearly shots and a checkup. If you could take him, I need to borrow some towels to clean up his accident in Jacob's truck."

Talking again to Charlie, Sarah says, "Oh, poor boy. Did his driving make you sick?" She takes the leash and gives me a towel.

Without comment, I turn and stomp back out to the truck. My head spins with questions, and my heart squeezes like a tightening vice from her betrayal. How can she act so uncaring? I'll never forgive her for breaking up with me that way. I wipe out the pickup floor and throw the towel in the garbage. Who cares if she might want it back? I pace around the parking lot, trying to calm down enough to reenter the office. This is crazy. It's Sarah. Regardless of how I feel about her, I'll need to finish this visit and take Charlie somewhere else next time.

But before I have a chance to go back in, Sarah and Charlie walk toward me around the side of the building. "Dad says no charge, this time. He wants to thank you for your service."

The wind whips Sarah's hair into her eyes, and she tucks it behind her ears. She hands Charlie's leash to me, and our hands touch. Sarah's eyes shine with glassy tears when she looks into my eyes. I look away.

"Tom, I'm so sorry. I wasn't thinking clearly, and I was so lonesome. There's no other excuse I can make except that I was too young to figure things out and angry with you for leaving me. Please forgive me." She wipes away the tears that spill down her cheeks. Charlie yips as if commiserating. She leans down and pets Charlie again, wiping her tear-stained face on Charlie's fur. "Hey, boy, you forgive me, don't you?"

I yank him toward the truck. "Tell your dad, thank you. We better get going. Lots to do on the farm today. Besides, you probably want to finish up here so you can see your fiancé tonight."

I open the passenger door, and Charlie jumps in, sitting as if he belongs there. Walking to the other side, ready to open the driver's side door, I stop when Sarah yells, "There is no fiancé. He couldn't replace you."

She turns and runs toward the front door of the office.

I hurry to catch her arm. "Sarah don't do this to me. Don't make me hope again." But my actions tell a different story. I fold her into my arms, and we stand holding one another, Sarah sobbing into my shoulder. I push her back after a bit and lift her face to mine.

"I love you, Tom. I never stopped loving you."

I don't respond. It's too soon to look beyond what happened, but my lips search out hers, and everything else in this world disappears.

Chapter 37

May-June 1964: Rev. DeJong

For weeks after VanVleet's body is discovered in mid-May, whenever a group in Stockwell gets together, the topic soon settles on the mystery of Gerrit's death. Most of the town gradually accepts that Gerrit fell on the pitchfork and bled to death. After a while, everyone moves on to other gossip, the uproar is forgotten, and life returns to normal.

On the day of Gerrit's funeral, the late May weather turns cool and cloudy. Rev. DeJong holds the funeral service with only a few fellow church members in attendance at the chapel. The eulogy he gives speaks to the living and shares no praises for the life VanVleet has lived. Rain pelts the car windows as DeJong and his wife drive to the cemetery, conditions typical of spring days in this part of the Midwest. Only the pallbearers and Pastor DeJong and his wife walk through the muddy ground to the readied grave under umbrellas, hiding their unfeeling faces. DeJong had asked for volunteers to be pallbearers, but only two men came forward. That morning, he made more calls and finally found six willing men.

It also falls to the pastor to deal with the VanVleet estate since they have no relatives close. The police found no papers in the house indicating what should be done with the farm. So Chief Borden called Rev. DeJong soon after the discovery of the body, asking him to hire a lawyer to find the two adopted kids and take care of their inheritance.

"The coroner is waiting to file the death certificate until all the evidence pointing to the time of death has been investigated," Chief Borden tells DeJong. "Getting a lawyer before the death certificate is filed will smooth the probate process for those kids. I think they deserve all that's available after what they went through."

"Seems like those kids should have been helped at the time," Rev. DeJong comments.

"We questioned some of your congregation a couple of times years ago, but everyone said the VanVleets were doing a wonderful thing taking in those two kids." Chief Borden's voice raises as he responds.

There's silence on the other end for a time.

DeJong concedes, "These Dutch stick together too much sometimes. Sorry, it was all before my time here. I shouldn't have criticized. Yes, I'll get a lawyer. It's the least I can do to set things straight."

"Could you also come in soon and give your formal statement? We're trying to tie this whole thing up as soon as possible." Pastor DeJong promises to come as soon as he gets a free afternoon. Both men hang up and move on to their day's busy workload.

Two weeks after the call, Rev. DeJong finally gets a free afternoon to visit the police station. He put it off until he could talk to the lawyer, not for himself, but to protect the VanVleet kids.

When he arrives at the station, Chief Borden and Officer Manning lead him toward the back of the building into a small room. They offer him coffee or water, but he declines. Chairs scrape as the three men settle into their spots, Rev. DeJong opposite both officers with a small table in-between.

"Wow, now I know what a suspect feels like. This is quite intimidating." DeJong tries to joke but feels his hands begin to sweat. No matter if he did nothing wrong, the situation makes him quite uncomfortable. He sits in silence while the officers consult their folders, turning pages of notes as they read.

The small gray room's ventilation system kicks on, making a hum in the background to
cancel the silence. One glass block window lets in filtered light, and the one light fixture above the table shines down without sending light toward the corners.

Before long, Chief Borden says, "We have most of what we need from you about the day you discovered the body. Here's a copy of what you told us so far. Could you please read it and tell us if there's anything you would like to add?" He hands the preacher a typed paper, and DeJong takes a few minutes to read it.

"I'd say that's about it. I can't think of anything else."

"If you could please sign it then. We have a couple more questions, and you'll be able to go." Chief Borden smiles, and DeJong takes a big cleansing breath.

Officer Manning stands and leans casually against the table. "I've been looking into the whereabouts of the VanVleet kids. I found a military record for a Tom

VanVleet with an address in Nebraska, showing a male of about the right age. Got any idea if it could be Gerrit's son? The service records show he was discharged not long ago."

Rev. DeJong feels his heart begin to race. He looks from Borden to Manning and down at his hands. He can't outright lie. "Yes, I believe it is," he says, looking straight at the two men. "His stepfather contacted me via his cousin who lives here in Stockwell, wanting to ask a few things about Gerrit and Alice and the sister, Catherine." The room closes in more. "I didn't say anything about this before because I didn't think it was important."

"Everything's important, Reverend, when it comes to an investigation," Borden says with another broad smile. He's up now, too, and puts his hand out to shake the pastor's hand. DeJong sees it as a signal for him to stand also.

"Thanks for your help," says Manning. "We'll be in touch if we need anything else."

Out in the fresh air, Rev. DeJong hurries to his car. Now is the time to make another call to Nebraska. Arriving home, Rev. DeJong rushes past his wife and into his study. "Got to make a call." She stands, hands-on-hips, wondering what the hurry is.

Dialing the number with shaking fingers and waiting for the line to connect makes DeJong pace as far as the phone cord will allow. The ringing on the other end becomes endless. Finally, a click on the line and a woman's voice makes the pastor's breath release.

"Hello, this is Emily speaking."

DeJong doesn't wait to ask for Jacob or Tom. His words spill out to Emily, "This is Rev. DeJong from

Stockwell. Wanted to call to tell Tom his foster father has passed away. They think it was an accident, but I'm afraid there'll be questions."

Emily makes no sound of surprise or shock. "Yes, Jacob's cousin called to tell us the news, but thank you for calling."

"That's not all. The Stockwell police found Tom through his military record. I'm sorry, but when they asked me about it, I had to collaborate and tell what I knew. I couldn't lie. So far, they haven't asked about Catherine, and I haven't said anything about where she is."

Emily's voice falters. "I'm sure you did what you had to do."

After the call, she hurries to the workshop to relay the messages.

Chapter 38

July 1964: The Police

The police question many of the parishioners from Rev. DeJong's church. Now that the VanVleets are both gone, the church members are more willing to talk about the situation concerning the young children the VanVleets had adopted. No actual proof surfaces, but past rumors are shared. The two children's lives are a tale of solitary days spent working whenever not in school. One former Sunday School teacher remembers seeing Catherine's bruised arm when her sweater slipped from her shoulder, exposing a sleeveless top. When she asked the girl what had happened, Catherine said she had fallen off her bike. A few other town residents tell similar stories, but sadly, no one had ever confronted the parents.

Three weeks after the initial investigation, the police receive the forensic report from the coroner. Using the state of the body's decomposition and the status of the insect population on the body, they approximate the time of death to be the last week of

April. The report states the cause of death to be a 'probable accident' until the investigation is concluded.

The discussion among the officers about the findings makes the small police station hum with suspicions. Accidental death is questioned.

Officer Manning stands to get a cup of coffee. "I still don't see how a guy could fall onto a pitchfork without someone causing him to fall with enough force to puncture his chest."

Jansen adds his thoughts. "That old guy, Gerrit was pretty emaciated. And if he tripped over a cat or something, I bet the tines would be able to puncture like they did."

Another officer adds, "Maybe he wanted to end it all and dropped down from the haybales onto the pitchfork."

Laughter and comments to be serious fill the small station. The room grows quiet again,
everyone thinking about the coroner's report and the scene.

Officer Manning stands and interrupts the calm. "Hey, listen to this. I've been checking military records and who we think is Gerrit's son, Tom, flew into Chicago from his tour in Vietnam and traveled by bus to Nebraska toward the end of April. That's about the same time VanVleet died."

Jansen adds, "And I found a police report from several years ago documenting an altercation the kid had with his stepfather before he left Stockwell."

"Guess it's time we find this Tom and question him," Chief Borden says.

Chapter 39

August-September 1964: Tom

The car I purchased at an auction for 'a song,' has become my project for the summer. Sarah joins in the activity whenever she can. Whenever Sarah isn't working at her father's veterinary office, she stands by and helps by handing me tools and holding parts, just so we can be together. Working on it together keeps my thoughts from wandering to past events.

Today, however, this partnership is causing me lots of frustration. "Sarah, look here. You can see this attachment slipped off. Didn't you hear all the clanking noise before it broke? It had to have made a lot of racket." Rubbing my hand through my hair, I shake my head.

"The whole thing clunks and rattles all the time. A new 'clank' didn't sound any different to me than the normal clanks." Trickles of tears streak through the dirt on Sarah's face. "You told me I was helping by taking it for a test drive around the barnyard, so you could listen to the engine."

Footsteps into the toolshed break the tension. "What's the problem? You two fighting again?" Jacob's belly laugh follows his words.

He walks over to check out what Sarah and I are peering at, and Sarah explains. "Tom is upset because I didn't hear a new clank in this old rattletrap."

"You know, Sarah, you're like my dad. He would plow up a field, not noticing the parts falling off until he ended up stuck in the middle of the field. 'Course, he wasn't far off from only working with horses. Never did get the hang of machinery."

"Guess all we can do is replace this part and try driving it again," I say, furrowing my brow. The moment turns when I smile at Sarah, and she wipes away the wet on her face with the back of her hands. When she looks up at Jacob and me, we both hold our hands in front of our mouths, trying to stifle laughter.

"What?" Sarah runs to the mirror hanging above the tool bench. "Oh, my."

I grab a hanky from my jeans and clean away some of the grime on her face. Out of the corner of my eye, I see Jacob exit the shed, so I take the opportunity to plant a kiss on Sarah's pouty lips.

"Hey, let's take a break on this old jalopy and see if Charlie wants to go for a walk."

Charlie's ears pop up, and he goes to stand at the door.

As we stroll along, the August sun beats down, but the tree-covered path to the creek always makes the day cooler. Showing his age, Charlie runs ahead, then sits down to rest to wait for us. Dry, soft earth beneath our feet shows through the browned grass, slowing our walk.

I kick up a cloud of dust. "All I hear from the farmers in the area centers on how much they need rain."

"Mmmmm," Sarah answers.

I know she's not thinking about the weather. All we both can think of is how soon she'll be leaving again for college. All summer, I let Sarah take the lead in our relationship. The hole inside my chest from our breakup has not completely healed, so I make no demands. My trust issue needs more time, but there's little time left. Before long, Sarah leaves, and our summer together will end.

We sit down in the grass along the creek while Charlie smells around the old trees. Sarah reaches over to take my hand. "Sorry I made more work for you. I know you want to finish the car, so we can take a drive in it before I leave for college, but I'll be home again before you know it for fall break."

I rub her hand, thinking back. "Jacob used to have an older tractor with spark plugs that were fouling up, causing the tractor to back-fire. They needed to be replaced, so he headed to town to buy spark plugs and said if it wouldn't start again, for me to take them out and scrub them up. That was supposed to fix the problem until he got back. He didn't tell me one spark plug at a time because each plug has its own spot where it needs to be. Taking them all out as I did can be quite a trick. If you don't put them back in the right pattern, connected to the right wires, the tractor won't start. It 'misfires.'"

Sarah laughs and says, "So the point of that story is?"

"I shouldn't have gotten mad at you. Everyone

screws up once in a while." I turn to look at Sarah. "And that's not my only mistake. Once when I was bringing in some bales of hay on the wagon, I drove way too fast and ..."

Sarah grabs my face and stops me mid-sentence with a kiss. Finishing my sentence falls by the wayside. My arms circle her waist, and before long, I push her down onto the grass, both laughing. Her long hair flips behind her in a fan, and she looks so beautiful. I find myself wanting to do more.

Coming to my senses, I pull off and flip back over to lay by her side. "No, Sarah. You're leaving in a week. This is not going to happen." I sit up but feel her hand on my back.

"If you would change your mind and come to college with me, we could see each other all the time."

"I told you, college isn't for me. Besides, you've only got two more years, and you can get a job teaching like you planned. So, we'll see if we both want to move forward when that happens."

Sarah stands to go. "You're so stubborn." She starts walking back toward the farmyard. "Come on, Charlie, let's race." She takes off at a sprint with Charlie running and barking beside her, rejuvenated with the hour's rest. I get up to go back but saunter along. Charlie thinks it's great fun to run back and forth between us. Will Sarah always be going ahead? Can I manage to keep up?

~

After Sarah leaves for college, we write often and also talk on the phone, but it isn't the same.

She assures me she can't wait to be home for fall break, but my insides feel like a balloon ready to burst most of the time when she's gone. My uncertain future, not only with Sarah, but also wondering when something will turn up concerning Gerrit's death makes me restless. The bubble is bound to burst any day now.

Good news comes when the lawyer Rev. DeJong hired gets in touch and informs me that Catherine and I will be inheriting the house, farm buildings, and sixty acres of farmland. But when I try to bring this up to Catherine to get her permission to give the lawyer her address, Catherine insists she doesn't want anything to do with it. So, the first thing I plan to do when the transaction is finalized is burn down that house and barn. After that, I'll either rent out the farm ground or sell the farm and give Catherine half the payment. If she refuses, I'll set up a bank account in her name, hoping someday she'll change her mind.

The second week of September, Jacob calls me to the phone just after getting out of the shower before breakfast. Dripping wet with only a towel around my middle, I walk into the kitchen. "Sorry, Tom, I think it's some police officer. Thought it might be important."

Jacob and Emily sit at the table, listening to the one-sided conversation. They look to me for an explanation as I hang up the phone. At first, I turn back toward the bathroom without sharing, but then I stop mid-step and look toward the couple. "They want to send someone out here to talk to me because I told him I couldn't leave with the harvest coming up. Guess maybe they want to talk some about Gerrit's death."

I return to my room to get dressed, leaving Jacob and Emily stunned, sitting in silence.

In late September, as the corn and beans are starting to dry and there's a promise of a great crop ahead, storms threaten the area. As the thunder booms and rain begins to hit the windows, Jacob and Emily pray after dinner for the storm to be light and for no damage to our crops. But as we sit watching TV that evening, the winds pick up, and warnings of local storms and straight-line winds flash across the screen. During the night, the old windows rattle, and branches hit the roof. I don't sleep well, and I hear Jacob and Emily moving about late into the night, also.

Before doing the milking, Jacob and I ride out to check our crops. Unfortunately, what we see is worse than what we imagined. The winds have knocked over the corn stalks making it impossible to move through the rows with the corn picker. The beans are also bent by the wind but not affected as much. The lines on Jacob's face deepen as we drive.

"Go ahead and yell at God. I wouldn't blame you. All you do is praise Him and look how He answers." I stomp on the pickup's gas, mad at the world.

"We've gone through bad times before; we'll get through this one," Jacob answers.

While working on a project in the toolshed, I settle down enough to think. While taking a short break, I sit down on an old tractor seat I've built into a chair and study the corn picker for a bit. An idea forms and my mental picture becomes something I'm sure I can construct. More ideas run through my head and that evening. I draw my plan out on paper.

"What's this?" asks Jacob, studying the drawing I flop in front of him.

"We're going to get that corn crop out. This plan shows how we can make an extension for each row of the corn picker that will separate the downed corn."

Emily walks over to the table to take a peek and listens. She puts her hand on my shoulder. "Do you think they'll work?" I give her a pinch, and Emily jumps back, chuckling. "Oh, sorry, didn't mean to doubt you."

Jacob pulls on his beard, thinking. "Regardless, if we can get the corn out now, the moisture content will be too high to be good for anything. Maybe some silage for our cows but selling part of our crop is usually our goal to pay for expenses."

I point to another drawing. "That's what this is for. We're going to build a corn dryer. We'll make one if we can't afford to buy one."

Jacob's smirk becomes a broad smile, and his eyes widen to saucer-sizes. "Tell me what we're going to do, boy."

~

Late one afternoon a couple weeks later, Jacob and I drive into the barnyard with another load of picked corn ready to put through the dryer. We constructed it using my design of a kerosene burner and a large fan to force hot air through the corn crib. Just as we finish with the load and get ready to drive back to the field to pick late into the evening, a police vehicle pulls up the driveway.

Chapter 40

September 1964: Tom

As the police car pulls to a stop, Charlie begins to growl and bark at the cruiser with an Indiana insignia on the door. Until I call him off, neither of the men inside attempts to exit the vehicle.

"Charlie, go lay down," I yell, but Charlie doesn't let up, so I grab him by the collar to hold him back.

The officer on the driver's side rolls down his window. "Safe to get out now?" He jokes. "That's a great guard dog you have there. We need him at our station in Indiana."

Charlie continues to emit a low growl, while I restrain him with a leash. Both officers open their doors, step out and extend their hands to me. "I'm Officer Manning, and this is Officer Jansen." They walk towards Charlie, but for once, his response is more barking instead of a wagging tail, so they stay put.

"Wow, feels good to stretch our legs. We've been driving since early morning."

Jacob walks over to the group, and I introduce him.

"This is my dad, Jacob." I see the look that shoots between the two men at his word, 'dad.' "Guess you figured out already that I'm Tom, the one you came to see."

Jacob shakes hands with both officers. "Come on in the house. Tom and I were about to take a coffee break anyway. My wife will be happy to have a couple guests."

Emily must have been watching from the kitchen window because when we enter the kitchen, she's already getting out the coffee cups. Her hand trembles as she pours the coffee. I catch her eye and smile, trying to calm her fears. But if policemen drive all the way from Indiana, could it be a friendly visit? Coming from that far away, they must think I have some information about Gerrit's death.

Emily shows the officers where they can freshen up and sets some cookies on the table still trembling. Her eyes meet mine, and she presses her lips together. I wink, and she can't help but smile back.

The men talk a little about the awful storm that came through and all the crops they saw down as they drove further west. Jacob's face breaks out in a huge smile when he talks about the innovations I've developed for us to get our corn out.

When the officers congratulate me, I look down and fidget with the cap I was wearing, now hanging on my knee.

"We're doing the same for our neighbors," Jacob says. "Tom is working on attachments for their corn pickers whenever he gets some time away from helping me. I don't know what we would have done if he hadn't figured this out."

Quiet settles, and the two officers look at each other. Manning asks. "Is there someplace we could talk privately with you, Tom? It might be better for everyone."

I smile and nod at Jacob and Emily. Having them worry about me is the last thing I want. I stand and lead the officers into the living room, where we can talk.

"It's about the circumstances around your father's death," Officer Manning says when they get far enough away from the kitchen.

Trying not to sound upset, I say, "He's not my father. I wouldn't ever claim that awful man as my father."

"Regardless, we still need to ask you some questions," Officer Jansen adds. Without being asked to sit, he plops down on the couch, leaning back and stretching out his legs on the footstool with a satisfying groan. Officer Manning and I each sit in one of the easy chairs.

My legs jump nonstop. "So, let's get this over with. What can I do for you, fellows?"

"Well," Officer Manning begins, "Given the bizarre circumstances of Gerrit's death, we're wondering if someone visited him who may have struggled with him and caused him to fall on that pitchfork. Do you have any idea who might have gone by the farm that day?"

My hands begin to sweat, and I feel like a heating pad might be under my legs. "No, can't say that I do. Haven't had anything to do with that place since I left when I was in high school."

Manning leans forward. "It's just that there was so much blood, more than normal for punctures like Gerrit received, and the odd direction the fork came through his body makes us question things."

Since I have no feelings for Gerrit, my face remains unreadable as both officers stare at me.

Jansen adds, "We've been doing some checking, and we noticed that you were on your way back to Nebraska about the same time your adopted father died. We know you traveled from Chicago to northern Indiana and switched buses. There was about two hours between your bus transports."

I laugh too loud and answer with a high-pitched voice, one I don't recognize as my own. "Gerrit's farm is a little far from that Howard Johnson's where I waited to change buses. Do you think I flew there and back to kill Gerrit?"

"No, but it stands to reason, if you could have a two-hour layover in northern Indiana, you could have done the same when the bus traveled past Stockwell, getting off for a short time and catching the next bus that came through, keeping about the same schedule. If we ask Emily and Jacob, maybe they'll tell us you arrived later than what they expected."

I stand and start pacing from one end of the living room to the other. "So, what do you want from me?"

"We need to see the boots you wore on your trip home. We found a partial footprint in the blood trail from Gerrit's body after moving the pitchfork."

This can't be happening. My heart beats like a racing auto. Could a small piece of evidence link me to being at the barn? I move like I'm made of rusty metal. "I'll have to get them from my bedroom."

The officers stand as if protecting the exit when I move to the bedroom door. Inside the room, I stare toward the window. It wouldn't take much to slide it open, hitch myself up and through, and run far from here. But Sarah's face enters my thoughts. Leaving her is not something I can consider, not now that our lives have become entwined again. I'll have to face whatever comes from this.

From the back of my closet, I grab the extra pair of army boots I brought home. Then hiding the pair, I wore home inside an old satchel, I toss it under my bed. Boots in hand, I walk back out and hand them to Officer Jansen. "You can search my closet if you want," I offer.

Jansen turns the boots over to see the underside and comments. "We'll have to compare these with the partial print. We need to take these back to Indiana with us. Is that a problem?"

"No, never wear my army uniform around here. Don't want to be reminded of some of the stuff I saw." Shaking my head, I lead them back into the kitchen.

Jacob and Emily stare toward the little group who emerge from the living room and wait for an update. But the three of us move without saying a word toward the door to the outside. I follow the officers into the barnyard toward their police car, my insides like mush.

"We'll be in touch," Officer Manning says as they climb into the cruiser. Charlie begins barking again as they turn the car and head back out the driveway.

I stand still for a moment, trying to decide how much to tell Jacob and Emily. The pleasant day has turned into a black tornado swirling with fear and hot frustration. I thought I had covered all my footprints. Had someone else been there and accidentally stepped in the blood? The only other person who might have gone there that day is Catherine. It's time to bring it up and see how she reacts. Then I can figure out how to proceed if the police return.

Opening the screen door into the kitchen, I plaster a smile on my face. "Ready to get back to work? Time's a-wasting."

Emily comes over to me. "Will those officers be back, do you think?"

I give her a big hug. "I hope not, but I don't want you to worry. They took my army boots to compare them to a partial footprint they found in Gerrit's barn, but there's no way it could match."

It wasn't a lie.

Staring at me for several seconds, Jacob grabs his cap. "Yep, better get back to work. That corn isn't standing up straighter anytime soon."

Chapter 41

October-November 1964: Tom

The days get shorter, and the cool fall air attacks the trees to produce a myriad of colors. Charlie and I have time again to take long walks along the path to the creek now that the corn is harvested and dried, ready to sell. Charlie runs a little slower this fall but retains his exuberance for checking under rocks and barking up trees if he spots a squirrel.

Enjoying the beautiful colors and breathing the earthy beginnings of vegetation decaying, I slacken to a pace even too slow for the aged dog. When Charlie returns to check on me, I stop and give him a round of pets and hugs, and Charlie bounds ahead, stopping at a spot not far along to turn and wait for me again. "All right, old boy. I get the hint."

Unwelcome thoughts swirl through my head as I amble forward. I've heard nothing from the police though they said they'd get back to me. When they find the boots don't match the partial footprint, hopefully, that will be the end of it. And they'll never find the actual pair I wore. When the Mulders were gone, I took those boots and burned them along with the other garbage in the burning barrel out by the barn. I'm still not sure if it's my footprint or Catherine's.

Talking with Catherine about the day Gerrit died proves impossible. Every time I try to bring it up, she changes the subject, talking about her college classes or how much she enjoys teaching her Sunday School class. After several weeks of calls, I've given up trying, hoping the whole thing will blow away with the coming winter winds.

A familiar car sits at the edge of the sidewalk when we return to the farmyard. Charlie runs faster than his old legs usually travel and barks his greeting. While running to keep up, the movement bounces my negative thoughts away and replaces them with visions of golden blond hair and full red lips. Seeing Sarah emerge from the house and run towards me feels like winning
the lottery without buying a ticket, just like the looks that pass between Jacob to Emily.

Our hug lasts for minutes, and I lift her in my arms and spin her until we both feel dizzy. Laughing, I bend down to kiss her waiting lips, never wanting to drag myself away. Finally, pulling back for air, I say, "I thought you wouldn't be home for fall break until tomorrow."

"My Friday classes were canceled, so I gathered my stuff and got out of there. All I could think of was getting here to see you. Haven't even been home yet."

Smiling at this news, I grab her hand and pull it to my lips. "Hey, my car is ready for another test drive. Had to fix something my girlfriend broke, but it's ready again."

Sarah's gentle slap on my arm shows she understands my teasing. It's been two months since we've seen each other, but we're back to feeling safe and comfortable together in a matter of minutes.

"I'll grab the key and tell Jacob and Emily we're taking a ride. Be back out in a bit. Come on inside, Charlie. You have to stay here."

I walk backward up the sidewalk, watching as Sarah heads to the workshop. My relationship with this girl, and the inner peace I see in the Mulders, even when hardship hits our lives, gives me a sense of a future full of hope. But when will my life settle into this same kind of quiet existence? The anticipation is the worst; waiting for Sarah to return home, waiting for the cops to notify me, and waiting for word from the lawyer.

Seated in the 56' Chevy passenger seat, my work in progress, Sarah smiles at me when I walk into the shop. Feeling as if my body is being pulled in two directions, I open the large overhead garage door and climb in behind the wheel. Telling Sarah about the police visit weighs on my chest but riding the country roads together comes first. It's what we've always done to find time to be together.

"Should we drive to your house and let your parents know you're home?" I glance her way. The look on her face tells me her parents still aren't crazy about us being together.

"I'm sorry, Tom. They'll come around. Let's not think about them and spoil our afternoon." Her hand finds my thigh. We drive in silence, the air whistling through the small opening in the windows, the only sound inside the auto for several miles.

On the open backroad, I push the accelerator to the

floor, and the car responds. Sarah yells, "Tom, slow down! This old car won't take this speed." She pinches my leg, and I let off the gas. Our laughter fills the small space. "You better let me drive if you're going to treat our car that way."

"Are you kidding? This thing will do whatever I need, and no, I'll keep driving, thank you. Where did you get the idea it's 'our' car, anyway?"

Sarah gives me another good-natured slap, and we fall into a playful rhythm. I talk about the harvest, our plans for the farm, and my talks with Catherine. I try to listen when Sarah shares a little about her classes and her work in one of the elementary schools near campus, but my thoughts keep wandering to having to tell Sarah about the recent police visit.

Driving back into the shed, I turn off the engine and pull Sarah close. "Have I told you yet, that I love you?" She tilts her head, and our kiss makes us both breathless. Sarah turns her body, and her soft curves send messages of future closeness. Her hand runs the length of my thigh, warming me all over.

"Tom, I've missed you so much. I'm tired of waiting." She turns more and begins to undo my jeans.

"Sarah, wait. There's something I need to tell you first."

Shifting back away from me, Sarah's eyes glisten, her eyelids half shut, her body wilting like
a neglected flower. Moving further toward her side of the car, she stammers, "What could be that important? This better be good."

I suck in air, and my voice comes out in a low whisper. "The police from Indiana came to see me a few weeks ago. They're investigating my adopted father's death. They claim it may not have been an accident."

Sarah's brows pucker. "What's that got to do with you?" I feel her eyes on me. I don't look her way. "Tom, you're scaring me. Tell me this is nothing we need to worry about." Sarah's voice rises as she speaks while wrapping her arms around herself.

"They have no proof. It's circumstantial stuff the police mentioned, but who knows with the cops? I needed to tell you, but I didn't want to write it in a letter." I open the car door and step out, the moment gone. "Come on, let's go help Jacob do the milking."

I take off toward the barn. Sarah catches up and grabs my hand. Our eyes meet in complete understanding. The message comes through; nothing can separate us.

The fall break weekend flies by, and after church on Sunday, Sarah prepares to drive back to college for her stay until the middle of December. Dr. and Mrs. Werner invite me to their home for lunch.

The space around the table feels so cold icicles could hang above from their fancy light fixture. My conversation becomes stilted. Sarah chatters away as if the gathering is an everyday occurrence, but my insides feel as icy as the inside of a meat locker.

After saying goodbye to her parents, I walk Sarah to her car. She clings to me, tears streaming down her cheeks. No words pass between us. I pull her arms from my neck and use my hanky to wipe away her tears. Opening her car door, Sarah gets in, but our hands remain linked together. With a glance toward the house and waving to her parents, I bend to give Sarah one last kiss. "Love you."

~

Without warning during the second week of November, I peek out my bedroom window when Charlie barks an alarm, to see the same two officers pull into

Officer Manning doesn't mince words. "Tom VanVleet, we are charging you with suspicion of murder. We have a warrant for your arrest. You need to gather some personal items and return to Indiana with us for your hearing."

Emily gasps and whimpers near the sink, and Jacob goes to her. They stand hugging one another. I do as I'm told while my insides melt. With shaking hands, I get my satchel and throw in some random items. I'll be leaving the safety of the Mulder's farm and going again to the unknown of the legal system, this time for a much more serious offence.

Chapter 42

November-December 1964: Tom

The prosecuting attorney turns out to be a guy I know from the church Catherine, and I attended with the VanVleets when we were young. Mr. VanWyk presents the case, laying out all the evidence against me for the Grand Jury. Although the case appears flimsy to me, my heart sinks when the Grand Jury votes to continue the charges against me.

The following day after the Grand Jury vote, Officer Manning escorts me to the courthouse again. A judge named Ketchum looks down from his bench over his wire-rimmed glasses. His bulbous nose and white hair show his numerous years of dealing with the criminal element. He clears his throat with several loud snorts. "Tom VanVleet, you are being charged with the murder of Gerrit VanVleet. How do you plead?"

I hear myself say, "Not guilty." The judge goes on to name my court date and other items that I don't zero in on.

"Your honor, I would like to speak with my client,"

comes a voice from the rear of the courtroom. I turn to see a young man not much older than myself. His uncombed hair hangs to within an inch of his shoulders, and his suit jacket is so short it doesn't cover his pants belt, but my breathing stills a little at the thought of someone else standing here with me.

He introduces himself as he plops is briefcase on the table. "I'm Jake. Jake Dobson. I'm the one who's taking care of your inheritance issues. So, I thought I may as well continue working for you with this case. That is if you want me to."

"Glad to finally meet you in person." While shaking Jake's small hand, my insides begin to calm. This nightmare may end up a happy dream after all, but first things first.

Jake explains, "Because you don't have money for bail and you refuse to have Jacob take out a loan, you'll have to stay in a small cell at the police station."

When Jake apologizes for this, I smile. "I hope Chief Borden's wife cooks as well as Sheriff McCloud's did."

Jake tucks his hair behind his ear and frowns. "You mean you've been in jail before?"

"Yeah, but that time it was for jumping a train to go west, peanuts compared to this."

~

After several weeks of Jake's friendly visits and my good-natured banter with the officers, I'm allowed some freedom not usually given to a defendant waiting to go to trial for murder. In the evening, the officer on duty joins me in my cell for a game of checkers, and Jake gets permission for me to call home and to Sarah's college apartment several times. Both Jacob and Sarah promise to be here when the trial begins.

I tell Sarah, "No, I don't want you to miss out on your classes." But it's like talking to a wall.

Due to the massive publicity associated with the case in the small town of Stockwell, the trial takes place in Henderson instead. The lawyers both hope to find a jury pool untainted by the media attention. Before the actual trial begins, the prosecutor files a request for evidence regarding the body's decomposition to be admissible. Jake objects, but the judge allows it.

My jury trial begins the first week of December with opening statements from both the prosecutor, Mr. VanWyk, and Jake, with their delivery looking different to the point of being comical. VanWyk's large belly slopes away from his chest, covered with a well-tailored suit. Jake's suit looks like he wore it in junior high. While the prosecutor bellows his words, spitting at all in line with the spray, Jake speaks in a monotone, reading most of his opening remarks.

The prosecution states, as expected, that I had reason to kill my adopted father. But, Jake tells the jury that Gerrit's death was an accident and that my behavior after the death shows I went about my life as normal, indicating I had no knowledge of Gerrit's death.

When VanWyk calls his first witness, Rev. DeJong, I turn to see Sarah and Jacob seated behind me to the right. They both give me tight smiles, but I can only stare. I draw on my military training to sit tall and show no emotion.

Rev. DeJong testifies, "I knew as soon as I got close to the barn, something was dead in there. I had experience with that smell while in the service."

DeJong also describes the odd placement of the body and the amount of blood he saw.

Jake asks in cross-examination, "Do you think it looked like Mr.VanVleet could have fallen on the pitchfork?"

The prosecutor objects, saying that would be opinion on the pastor's part. The judge does not allow the answer. When the next witness comes forward, my hands begin to sweat though I keep my outward appearance calm. The bus driver testifies to the time and day he let me off his bus even though it was against company policy.

"And why did the defendant say he needed to leave the bus?" asks VanWyk.

"He said he wanted to visit the place where he grew up. He was still dressed in his Army uniform, and I have a soft spot for military guys, so I broke the rule."

The most damning evidence comes when the forensic entomologist, Neal Haskell, explains, "Entomological evidence is the most accurate information to determine the time of death once a body decomposes. The insect species present at the body site indicates the body's long-term presence in the barn."

He pinpoints the time of death as the same time that I returned home from the service. All eyes from the jury stay glued to me, but I ignore their stares.

The coroner is called to the stand and explains that the pitchfork would not have done as much damage to the ribcage without external force. "I am sure the amount of bleeding was much more excessive than if only small punctures were made by a body falling on the pitchfork."

When the prosecutor finishes presenting his case

and rests, I slip a note to Jake. *Why didn't they bring up the boot mark?*

Jake shrugs, more preoccupied with his next move. He stands when the judge acknowledges the defense table and says, "I move that Tom VanVleet be acquitted on the grounds that the prosecution has not met the burden of proof. There has been no evidence submitted showing that Gerrit VanVleet was murdered." But Judge Perry denies the motion and directs the defense to be ready to continue the following day.

That evening, Sarah and Jacob are allowed to visit separately in my small jail cell. I ask about Emily when Jacob comes in, and he gives me a bear hug. "Actually, that hug's from her. She wanted to come, but someone had to stay back at the farm. Emily insisted I come to support Sarah. She's taking this pretty hard, so now I'm going to let Sarah have most of the time available to visit with you." He stops and wipes his eyes. "So, I'll see you again tomorrow in court." He gives me an over-the-shoulder hug and says, "We love you, kid. Can't wait for you to be back home." Jacob bangs on the cell door to leave.

Sarah's visit slashes my heart into tiny pieces. She tries to smile, but tears fall instead. Holding her close only makes things worse. Knowing our time is limited, I search for something to say to turn things around. "Sarah, I am so sorry. Your parents won't ever respect me when I get out of this. They'll never come around now."

"I don't care what they think, Tom. And you shouldn't be worrying about them now. We've got to think of a good reason you wanted to get off that bus. Maybe you could say you thought you'd left something valuable at the VanVleets." Sarah's thoughts tumble from her mouth like a waterfall. "You've got to make people believe you didn't go into that barn."

I grab Sarah's wrist. "I can't make up stories, Sarah. It will be worse if I get accused of lying under oath. No, we've got to trust Jake on this and pray there's not enough evidence to convict."

Too soon, Officer Manning comes to let Sarah out, saying Jake is waiting to speak to his client. With a final kiss, Sarah wills herself to smile and waves at me as she leaves.

Jake sits down on the cot as I pace. "Why didn't they enter the footprint into evidence? It's the one piece of evidence that would clear me for sure."

Shuffling through papers, Jake gives up after several minutes. "There's nothing in my files about the footprint. Are you sure they told you they found one?"

I run my hand through my thick hair. "Yes, when they came to talk to me the first time. That's why they wanted my army boots, to check if they matched the footprint."

"We'll wait and see how things go tomorrow, but if they don't mention the footprint or give us information about it, this whole trial could be thrown out of court. The prosecutor is required to provide us with all the evidence, even if it may hurt your case. It's called exculpatory evidence."

My face lights up. "That's the best news I've heard in weeks."

Jake sighs. "Yeah, well, in the meantime, we've got to get busy and go over our defense for tomorrow. Just so you know. I subpoenaed your sister, Catherine, for tomorrow's defense."

"What? No! I don't want Catherine involved."

"Too late. Besides, she was the one who called me and insisted."

Chapter 43

December 1964: Tom

Feeling groggy after the late-night session with my attorney and trying to sleep on the lumpy cot, I sit up and stretch when I hear talking in the offices out front.

It's Catherine's voice. "It's important that I see him before he goes to the courtroom."

Chief Borden answers, "Guess it will be okay, but make it short."

Trying to make myself more presentable, I jump up to splash some cold water on my face and run my fingers through my hair. I haven't seen Catherine since our visit on my way home from the army, although our weekly phone calls have kept us close.

The chief unlocks the cell door, and Catherine charges in to hug me. Her long dark hair is pulled back in a low ponytail, and she wears no makeup, but she looks great to me.

As soon as we're alone again, she says, "We have to talk."

I lead her to the cot, the only spot to sit together. "This is a mess, isn't it? After everything we went through at the VanVleets, we're still suffering because of them." I put my arm around Catherine, rubbing her back. "I didn't want you to get involved with this. Everything's going to turn out fine. They don't have any real evidence."

Catherine's brows pull together, and her eyes become slits. "I'm so worried about saying the wrong thing on that stand. I know I'll break if they ask me anything about my past with Gerrit, but Jake thinks some information about our past treatment by the VanVleets may sway the way the jurors think. I'll do anything to help your case. I know you didn't murder Gerrit." Our eyes meet, and I see something there made of sharp spikes and bristles. How can she be sure?

We sit holding each other for several minutes. "Can I ask you something about the day we met on my way home from the army?"

Catherine nods. "Sure, anything, Tom."

"Why did you turn south rather than north when leaving the gas station? Were you planning to go visit the VanVleet place?"

Catherine stands and walks toward the cell door, her back to me. "No, I got confused for a bit, and a mile down the road, I had to turn around and go back north."

Her added chuckle sounds forced. Why would she lie about this?

Chief Borden turns the corner into the cell area. "Time to go before long, Tom. Better get yourself cleaned up."

Catherine gives me another quick hug. Not looking me in the eye and with head down, she hurries out of the cell.

~

December winds blow and rattle the old windows that line the courtroom walls as I'm escorted into the mahogany-paneled room. White painted walls behind the judge's bench form a welcome contrast to all the rich, but dreary wood paneling. Unfortunately, no sunshine streams through the glass today. Light fixtures supply much-needed brightness. A storm brews inside and out while stragglers file into the spectators' seating. The bailiff seats the jury, and all are asked to rise as Judge Perry takes his place behind the judge's bench. Feet scuffling and chairs scraping, the only sounds heard as people again sit.

My defense begins with Jake calling another forensic entomologist who disputes the previous claims of the prosecution's entomologist. He says, "The stage of the insects on the body indicate Gerrit fell on the pitchfork many days before the defendant made his way to Nebraska across Indiana."

Mr. VanWyk has no questions. It's one man's testimony against another's.

When Jake calls Catherine as his next witness, I turn and grab her extended hand as she walks by to the table where I'm sitting. I mouth the words, "Be strong," and Catherine nods.

After some preliminary questions, Jake stands close and talks in a conversational tone.

"Catherine, when you met with Tom on April seventeenth, did he mention anything about going back to the VanVleet farm?"

Looking straight toward the jurors, she answers, "No, we didn't talk about our adoptive parents or the farm. We only talked about our futures."

Jake warned her he would be bringing up some difficult items, so he asks, "Was there a reason you didn't want to talk about the VanVleets?"

Catherine's body stiffens. She holds her hands tightly in her lap and stares toward me. In a shaky but strong voice, Catherine says, "Yes, Gerrit and Alice were abusive to us from the time we stepped foot on that farm. They were awful people."

I exhale a huge sigh when I hear the prosecutor's decision not to ask Catherine any questions. She would break if he asked her about Gerrit raping her. Standing up, Catherine sways and grabs the rail.

"Miss VanVleet are you okay?" the judge asks. The courtroom hums with concern as she nods to the Judge, while Jake helps her down and accompanies her to her seat.

After Jake questions the coroner and Chief Borden about specific days and times, he introduces a time and date flowchart showing the defense's estimate of the time of death compared to my movements last spring. No lines intersect. Jake rests his defense.

The following day, on December 14, the state and the defense give their closing statements bringing together their arguments before the jury. I watch each juror's face as Mr. VanWyk recounts their scant evidence in his booming voice. He paints a picture of a defenseless old man attacked by his young son, who hated the man for how he treated him and his sister.

Jake has no notes this time and gains confidence as he speaks. He imagines for the jury a different scenario. "Could there be the possibility that the feeble Gerrit VanVleet may have tripped over his own feet? Or perhaps one of the cats ran through his legs and caused him to fall backward onto the pitchfork. Either situation could cause a large amount of blood because of the force of the fall." He pauses for effect. "Both Tom and Catherine have overcome the treatment they endured from the VanVleets and now live productive lives, unconcerned with what happened on the VanVleet farm. Let them continue their paths of success with a not guilty verdict."

Turning my body toward the spectators, I catch Sarah's eye. She smiles through glistening eyes as she holds tight to Jacob's arm. She mouths the words, "I love you," holding her free hand over her heart. I nod and turn back facing the jury.

Judge Perry charges the jury with the job they need to carry out. He hits his gavel one time and adjourns the court, and the room empties to wait for the verdict.

Back in my cell with Jake, I perform a few jumping jacks to use up some energy. In short, breaths I ask, "Why didn't you bring up the footprint? Thought you said we could get this thing thrown out."

Jake joins in the exercises, panting. "Let's wait to see how the jury decides. If they say guilty, that will be the time to bring it up and ask for a mistrial. If it's not guilty, there's no point. You'll be on your way back to Nebraska." He stops exercising and faces me. "Not so sure I want to bring it up. Wondering why you're so sure it would clear you."

I continue exercising ignoring Jake's last comment.

There's no decision by evening, so Jake leaves and says he'll be back in the morning. Sarah and Jacob stop by for a short visit trying to be positive, talking about the upcoming children's pageant at church and what fun it will be decorating the trees together for Christmas at our respective homes.

I can't sleep thinking about what I'll be facing in the morning. Pacing the cell from one end to the other becomes my burden. About midnight, I hear the sound of sirens and loud voices in the outer offices.

"Hey, what's going on?" I yell to the guards.

"The house and barn out at the VanVleet farm are on fire. No one reported it until it was too late, and both are beyond saving," the officer barks, trying to speak above the noise of the sirens.

Finally, laying down, outrageous thoughts converge into my awareness. Could Catherine have had something to do with the fire? Legally, the farm is ours to do with as we please. Jake had finished the transfer of ownership before the beginning of my trial, so other than causing the fire department problems, no one can charge Catherine if she did do it. Those thoughts make me smile. The buildings that represented so much cruelty, are gone for good.

The dawn's light streaming through the small cell window gives me a sense of peace. Calm fills my chest. Before long, Jake arrives to join me for breakfast and he agrees, the property is ours to do with as we please.

After another eight hours of deliberations, we receive word that the jury has reached a verdict. Everyone interested in the outcome returns to the courthouse. A quiet settles over the room when the foreman is asked to deliver the verdict. He hands a paper to the bailiff, and he passes it to Judge Perry to read. The judge's face remains blank. The paper is returned to the foreman. Judge Perry says, "Tom VanVleet, please stand."

I feel Jake's arm under my elbow as we stand together.

"Not guilty of all charges, Your Honor," the foreman calls out.

Chapter 44

December 1964: Tom

It's late afternoon when Jacob and I walk into the kitchen, back at the farm in Nebraska. Charlie barks and runs circles around us. Emily turns from the stove and, without greeting, breaks into tears. I hurry to her side. "We're back, and it's time for you to take it easy." Leading her to the table, I point to a chair. "Sit, while I finish making dinner."

Jacob hugs his wife and takes a seat too, exhausted. Slumped shoulders replace Emily's usual spunk, and Jacob seems to be moving much slower. The last few weeks have aged them both. I vow to make it up to them. After eating, I insist on cleaning up while they relax.

"Is there anything else I can do?" I look from one to the other, my insides churning with regret. How can I ever repay both for all they've done?

Emily sighs as if a burden has been lifted. "The milking will need to be done later, but I'm thinking it's about time we get the boxes of Christmas decorations down. I know Sarah wants to help decorate the tree, but we can get the rest of the items put out before she comes home for Christmas break next week. I think I'd like to add a little cheer to the house."

"Great idea," says Jacob. "Come on Tom. You can climb up in the attic and hand them down to me."

~

The following day after the milking and breakfast, Emily and I bring the boxes of decorations into the living room and begin unpacking. I'm vibrating with excitement, even at my age. Christmas had never been a happy time at the VanVleets, just another day. Sometimes Alice baked a cake, and we celebrated Jesus' birthday, but no Christmas tree or lights adorned the inside of the VanVleet's house. Catherine and I were given new socks and maybe some mittens, but never toys or candy. This Christmas will be the total opposite. To the Mulders, the holidays mean bright lights, baking and gift-giving.

"Where'd Jacob go? Thought he wanted to help decorate." I pull out a humongous wreath and start to fluff up its smashed branches.

"I can't make that man settle back and relax for anything. He gets something in his head that needs to be done and he has to do it right away. He said something about cleaning out the burn barrel by the barn before we have to use it again with all the Christmas clutter."

The wreath nearly drops from my hands. I feel the blood drain from my face and my knees feel as if they might buckle. When Emily looks up, I try to smile, but she sees through the attempt. "What's the matter? You look like a ghost walked into the room."

Setting the wreathe down on the coffee table, I make up an excuse to go outside to help Jacob. Emily stands there, her eyes wide with surprise. She calls after me, "Well, my, everyone's deserting me."

Snow has fallen during the night, making the tree branches look like shimmering white arms ready to grasp any passerby. But the beauty of nature becomes trivial as I hurry to the side of the barn to find Jacob. He stands with shovel in hand, digging at the ashes left in the burn receptacle. A wheelbarrow sits next to the barrel, partially full of dull crusty ashes.

I call out, "Hey, Jacob, why didn't you ask me to do this? It's such a nasty job."

Jacob turns when he hears me. He holds a shovel full of ash and burn debris. In the middle of those ashes is part of a badly burned black boot. For a moment, we both stand there taking in the awful truth. Jacob lowers the contents of the shovel into the wheelbarrow. He takes a huge breath, and his head drops to his chest. When he peeks up at me, his brow has become a field of furrows, his eyes narrowing so much, it's a wonder he can see.

"Well, Tom, what do you have to say for yourself? Why would you burn your army boots?"

A light snow begins to fall again, as if trying to cleanse the air of doubt. I grab the shovel. "They kill my feet every time I wear them and besides, they remind me too much of all the stuff from Vietnam."

After what seems like an hour, Jacob's head bobs up with a broad smile plastered across his face and his laugh lines give him an impish expression. He shakes his head. "Sorry to even question. Should have known better."

"No problem. Hey, I'll finish this. Emily needs help with some decorating," I say, starting to dig at the low contents left in the barrel.

Jacob grabs the wheelbarrow handles. "Kind of why I was out here." He chuckles to himself. "She can never decide where to hang things and I have to stand around waiting until she does." He begins to push the wheelbarrow. "We'll finish together. I'll dump this load. Loosen the rest of the ash and it'll make it easier to shovel out. One more load and we can both go back into the house. Maybe by then, Emily'll have decided where the decorations should go this year."

Shoveling the rest of the ashes, I think back to my quick answer. If I had stammered and faltered coming up with a good reply, what would Jacob have done? I need to be prepared in case the topic of the bloody footprint ever does come up, but with the house and barn burned down to the ground no more investigation is possible. Catherine only smiled when I asked if she had done the deed.

We both agree the place needs to be sold, so bad memories can vanish along with the sale. Jake says the farm may be worth a little more now because a buyer won't have to dispose of the dilapidated buildings.

The Christmas celebration this year tops anything I have ever experienced. Sarah spends her
first weekend home from college decorating the tree at the Mulders with Emily. Jacob and I sit back and give advice. Carols sing out from the record player and on those with high notes, Charlie tries to croon along. The dog loves all the hubbub and plays fetch with the new chew toy Sarah bought for him.

I am not invited to Sarah's house to decorate, but

Sarah assures me not to worry. "My parents want time alone with me. They want the decorating to be just our little family, like it's always been."

A storm threatens on Christmas Eve. The radio blares all morning in the kitchen while Emily cooks and tries to catch the weather report. Expecting Catherine any minute to make it here through the storm makes us all tense. Snow begins to come down in huge flakes and every few minutes one of us goes to the window to look out. Charlie can't settle down. He jumps up and goes to the door and whines each time we make a move.

Inside the warm kitchen, the oil stove chugging out heat gives the room a cozy feeling. Emily's brow glistens with perspiration from the additional oven heat and all the food preparations.

After everyone arrives, we plan to have a massive meal at lunch, followed by an afternoon visit. After a light dinner, we'll drive to town for the Christmas Eve service. We're praying the weather will not interfere with our plans.

"She's here," I call out and Charlie and I run out into the cold to help Catherine with her bags.

~

Waking up from a deep sleep, I overhear Catherine and Jacob talking in the kitchen. I sit up and rub the sleep from my eyes. My back aches from sleeping on the couch this whole week while Catherine's been visiting. The upstairs bedrooms are too cold for a guest to be comfortable during the winter, so I gave up my bedroom on the main floor for her where it's warm.

"Don't you think it's puzzling that the police asked for his army boots, but the prosecutor never brought them up for evidence during the trial?" I hear Jacob ask.

I strain to hear Catherine's reply.

"Yeah, but it doesn't matter. The jury acquitted him and that's the important thing. If there was a matching footprint, it's gone now." Catherine emits a rueful snicker. "Someone took care of that."

"You're right. Guess I should be glad."

I walk in and join the two at the table for coffee before going to do the milking. Quiet settles over the room as we each reflect on the previous conversation.

Catherine places her hand on my arm. "I'll be leaving later in the day. Got to get back to all my obligations."

Frowning, I say, "I don't want you to go, but I know you have to."

Catherine smiles my way, and I try to put on a happier face.

Chapter 45

January 1965: Tom

The winter doldrums settle into the Mulder household. With Sarah back at college and Catherine's return to Michigan for her work and studies, my routine leaves little to excite. The higher corn prices along with the new options I designed to get out the damaged crop, have made up for the corn lost after the storm. So, Jacob and I work at ordering seed and fertilizer for spring and also order much needed supplies for repairing fences and fixing the chicken coop.

On a frigid day in late January, we're in the barn chopping ice from the waterers when Jacob says out of the blue, "You know, Tom, if you ever want to get anything off your chest, I can be a good listener. The frown you often wear makes me wonder what's going in that head of yours."

I stop working. "No, don't think I need to talk about anything. I'm missing both the girls, especially Sarah, so maybe that's causing me to look this way. Once Sarah's finished with college, I'm going to ask her to marry me."

Jacob smiles and starts chopping again. "That's great Tom. With the money you make off selling that farm in Indiana, you'll be able to buy a nice ring and invest in some farmland of your own around here. But I want you to know, you're always welcome to work here at this farm and when we're gone, it will be yours."

"Thanks, but I don't think we'll have to worry about changing anything on this farm for a long time."

Working side by side with Jacob day after day warms any cold spot I ever felt in my short life. Jacob and Emily's influence continues to show in my life. One of my teachers used to compare people's feelings to bedsprings by saying, "No matter how many times they're used, they snap back if shown the love they deserve." I'm living proof of that statement. You should never judge someone by their relatives.

I wake from my thoughts when Jacob smashes into the layer of ice on one of the waterers with an extra amount of force. Looking up I see my benefactor clutch his chest, a stricken look covering his face. Time freezes as I look on, unable to move. Jacob collapses, first to his knees and then his body slumps over onto the cold, barn floor. I wake from my shock and kneel beside the big man, lifting Jacob's head to rest on my knees.

"Don't leave us, Jacob. You've got to hang on. I'm going to run to the house to get Emily. We'll call the ambulance and get you to the hospital."

With a strength I didn't expect, Jacob grabs my jacket to pull me closer to his mouth. "Tom, keeping secrets will eat at your soul. Jesus forgives all."

Tears stream down my face as Jacob fades. "What

do you mean?"

"The burned boots. Do they match that footprint?" Jacob gasps out the words.

I hug him and rock the old man in my arms. Jacob's breathing catches, becomes steady, stops again for a moment. "Guess we'll never know now." I straighten. "I've got to get help. Hang on."

I let Jacob down as gently as possible and race to the house. I run in and grab the phone and when Emily sees my face, she knows. She hurries out to the barn, not stopping to take a coat.

The operator connects me to the hospital in town. Waiting for a reply makes my insides feel like a tornado churning and gaining momentum, the longer it takes. The nurse who answers takes my information and explains the ambulance is already on its way. I pray it will get here in time, but the snow-covered roads will make traveling slow.

When I hang up, I snatch Emily's winter coat and hustle back to the barn. Charlie had
followed Emily and stands at the barn door barking, knowing something is not right.

Squeezing between the opening of the door to keep Charlie at bay, I store the scene before me in the recesses of my mind, etching it there, never wanting to forget. Emily is lying on the barn floor facing Jacob, holding him as close as possible, her face against his, and repeating the words, "I love you, don't leave me. I love you, don't leave me."

I walk close and cover the two lovers with Emily's coat. We're suspended in time until I hear the ambulance siren a good thirty minutes after my call.

~

The January weather breaks for a couple hours for Jacob's funeral. It's as if God looks down to arrange the setting for one of His saints. My pain is magnified knowing Jacob died having doubts about my innocence. Being surrounded by all the females in my life helps me cope. Sarah and Emily sit on either side of me, and Catherine's arm protects Emily two seats over. I need to stay strong for all these women. But the message the pastor gives of a life lived as Jesus would have us live, makes my heart tear inside my chest, and I break down at one point. I promise myself, no matter what, I'll live to honor Jacob's memory.

The next few days, I want to make sure the farm runs like Jacob has always done. I try to discuss business with Emily, but she's too distraught. She sits alone in Jacob's big chair in the living room, only coming out when either Sarah or Catherine insists she comes to eat the meal they prepared.

On the following Monday, Sarah throws her arms around me once more before returning to college. She reminds me, it's only five weeks until spring break. Catherine gets permission from her two professors to stay another week, her class load only being part-time.

We reconnect as Catherine helps me with some of the chores. We finally are able to talk
about the events we endured at the VanVleet place, and it helps put away some of our negative feelings.

Chapter 46

February 1965; Tom

One February day the sunshine returns as bright as a hero home from war. Catherine needs to return to Michigan soon, so, after the lunch dishes are cleaned up, I ask, "How about we go for a ride in my old Chevy? We could both use a little down time."

Catherine smiles. "Thought that car was reserved only for Sarah."

"I bet Sarah would say it's okay." I wink and go tell Emily we'll be gone for a short time and give her a reassuring hug.

The old car still has its definite shakes and rattles, so once we're out on the backroads, I slow down so we can hear each other better. "Are you ever going to tell me if it was you that burned down the house and barn? You know I'm fine with it."

Catherine stares my way, hangs her head, her voice soft and muffled. "Yes, I had to get rid of that horrible place. Too many bad memories. Besides, after Jake told me about the bloody footprint, I couldn't have them investigating there anymore."

I slow down even more, back into a field road and shove the car into park. "Wait, why were you so worried about the footprint?"

When Catherine raises her head, her eyes are red-rimmed, and her hands shake when she pushes her hair behind her ears. "I would have come forward if you had been convicted, I swear." Her words fall out like a torrent in a river. "I went to the farm after I left you that day we met. I wanted to make Gerrit pay, but things went terribly wrong." She wipes her cheeks with her sleeve and sighs.

I rub my chin, thinking about how to continue. "You went there on your own? Why didn't you ask me to come with you?"

Catherine doesn't answer. I reach over to grab her hand. "Okay, so, can you talk about how he ended up with the pitchfork through his chest?"

As if relieved to get it off her chest, Catherine spills out more words. "When I got there, I went into the house first, but didn't find anyone. I literally flew out to that old, dilapidated barn, thinking I needed to find him before I lost my nerve. I wasn't planning to hurt him, just scare him into thinking I would. Gerrit had been working in the barn and didn't hear me pull up. I peeked around the half-open door of the barn, hoping to see something to grab for protection before going too far in, but I had to stop to let my eyes adjust."

I stare her way. "I wish you hadn't put yourself in that danger."

"Just let me finish." Catherine takes a deep breath. "After a few more steps, I spotted the pitchfork. I grabbed it, but just then a rat ran by my feet and a big yellow cat ran after the rat. You know how much we've each hated those rats. I couldn't help myself, I screamed and dropped the pitchfork making more noise. Gerrit yelled, 'Who's there?' He came around the corner, and I was standing face to face with him." She sniffles and uses both hands to swipe away tears. "He had the nerve to say, 'So, you've finally come back. It's about time.' Like I would've wanted to see him. His awful voice made me nearly run back to my car."

Catherine's whole body shakes as she's talking. I squeeze her hand to reassure her. "I leaned over and snatched the pitchfork, but I lost my balance when I bent over, stumbled and almost fell, still holding the pitchfork. Gerrit plodded toward me and tried to yank the pitchfork out of my hands. Using all my strength, I pulled back on the handle. It was like a tug-of-war, but I finally lost my grip. The fork flew with a clunk behind Gerrit with the tines up. He fell backwards, tried to grab the post of a nearby stall, but instead fell onto the fork."

Catherine sobs to herself. I clear my throat, not sure what to say, but move closer to hug her.

She goes on in a soft voice. "The tines tore through his skinny chest, and blood covered the front of his shirt and spilled onto the floor. I got so scared, I ran from the barn, maybe stepping in the blood. But I guess I was still thinking clearly because I made sure I stayed on the grass so I wouldn't leave footprints."

She lays her head against my shoulder, spent from telling the tale, then adds, "Sometimes I can still hear his cries, calling to me from inside the barn."

Again, Catherine stops to catch her breath and wipe her wet eyes. I hold her, waiting for her to finish. "I ran to the car as fast as I could. Thank heaven it started with no problem. I shoved it into reverse and backed out of the driveway, my hands shaking inside the gloves I was still wearing. My whole body went into a cold sweat. I yelled, 'Oh God, did I kill him?' and screamed for several miles as I drove away. Later when I calmed down, I realized it was a freak accident, and no one could track me for having been there since I was wearing those gloves. I didn't realize I might have stepped in the blood. It was spreading everywhere."

My heart races. Jacob enters my mind telling me to be truthful. I've got to tell someone, and Catherine will never go to the police and report the information. I don't think I can be tried again, anyway, so I say with all the persuasion I can muster, "You didn't step in the blood. I probably did. I went to the VanVleet place, too, that same day and must have gotten there a short time after you left."

Catherine wipes her eyes and sits up straight. "What? But you didn't go in, right?"

"I did much more than look around the farm like Jake indicated at my trial, and I did talk the bus driver into letting me off. When I got to the farm, Gerrit was still alive. He begged me to go get a doctor but helping the situation along seemed like a better choice. He was a goner anyway. Saw plenty of similar cases in Vietnam. So, I put both feet on the handle of the pitchfork and jumped down hard. More blood squirted from the punctures and Gerrit screamed in agony," I say without feeling. "I'm not sorry I did it."

Catherine squeezes my hand now and turns to look at me.

"I told him, this pain is nothing like what you caused Catherine. You deserve every bit of it."

Catherine nods in agreement.

"He begged me again to get help, but I said, 'you never helped us.' I showed him my Distinguished Service Cross, for bravery beyond the norm and told him it was no thanks to him and Alice." I stop to take a breath, looking into Catherine's eyes for approval, and go on. "I jumped on the pitchfork a few more times, yelling, 'may you burn forever' as loud as I could, but he didn't rouse. When I left there, I wasn't sure Gerrit was dead, but I was sure he would be before long."

Catherine holds my hand even tighter. "So, I would say, we're in this together, and we both got our revenge."

We sit in silence for several minutes before I move over again and start the car to continue our silent ride.

Epilogue: Tom

I am alone now. Sitting and staring out the nursing home window each day, anticipating the reunion with those I love who've gone before me. I'm eager to join Sarah, the love of my life, Catherine, my dear sister, and Emily and Jacob, the strangers who became everything to me.

I ask myself every day why Sarah had to go before me. She shared her light with so many through her teaching. She became a mother to our three children and hostess to our kids' many friends who spent hours roaming our farm and playing near our beloved creek. Our time together ended after fifty beautiful years, but too soon as far as I'm concerned. She still had so much to offer. Sarah never stopped believing in me, so I couldn't bring myself to share my story of guilt with her. I couldn't bear to see that same doubt in her eyes as I'd seen in Jacob's.

Cancer took my sister Catherine's life before she had a chance to marry and have more children. For a short time, she tried to find the baby she had given up for adoption, but when the trail ended, she decided to trust that God had taken care of the child. Before her diagnosis, teaching became her way of dealing with her former hate. The love she shared with so many children over the years healed her inner spirit and eventually helped her to forgive. Our children looked forward to the visits from Aunt Catherine at Christmas and for a week every summer. She became a remarkable influence in their lives.

When Jacob died, I lost my mentor and the only person I wanted to call Dad. Eventually, I learned to live with the fact that Jacob may have had doubts about my innocence. Jacob encouraged me to be truthful because he knew the lies would eat away at my strong character and bring me down. However, Jacob couldn't have looked ahead to see the meaningful relationship I would develop with Emily. After Emily's grieving changed from sadness to remembering the joy she and Jacob shared, she and I had many evening talks that helped both of us to heal.

After many months of sharing, I finally told her my story of revenge. Emily opened her worn Bible and proved to me that I could again be innocent because of Jesus' sacrifice. All I needed to do was ask for forgiveness.

I learned to forgive the VanVleets and myself for my act of revenge. It was difficult, but with Emily as guide, the path to forgiveness involved adding more and more love inside my heart and shoving the hatred farther away. Each child Sarah and I added to our home and each adventure we shared over the years helped with the healing process. By helping others who needed our care, our lives became so full of love and joy that bitterness had no place. After turning the farm over to Jed and Mary, our son and daughter-in-law, Sarah and I found new purposes by working for our church, visiting the sick, welcoming new family members, teaching Bible classes, and chauffeuring those who needed transportation to doctor visits.

I learned that God has a plan for each person; a plan for celebration, not judgment; a plan for joy, not sorrow; a plan for peace, not fear, if only we allow God to take over and quit resisting.

When I think back over my life's journey, many people helped me make my way; the truck drivers who let me hitch a ride, the old farmer who took me in with no questions asked, the young lawyer who helped me gain my freedom, and of course Jacob and Emily. They all served as my angels here on earth when I needed help the most. I had promised to return the favor when I parted with some of these angels, and I tried to do that over the years. Sarah and I never got rich with monetary rewards, but we earned many treasures that no miser will ever experience, by repaying kindness for kindness.

Today I'm waiting for a special celebration. It's my eightieth birthday, and my daughter Laura, and her husband, Mike, will be arriving before long to take me to the church for my party. Everyone, including my three children, six grandchildren, and fourteen great-grandchildren, plus their significant others, plan to attend along with many church friends. I wanted a small get-together with just family, but they wouldn't hear of it. Finally, I agreed to their plans with one stipulation. They must drive me past my farm, inherited from Jacob and Emily, now belonging to my older son, Jed, and his wife, Mary. They've remodeled the house, making it look more modern, but the old barn still stands, as it was when I slept there for many nights before moving into the house.

Over the years, that barn has gone through many changes. When it was young and new, it could take on any storm, fight off diseases, and produce a good amount of product. The boards began to shrink as the barn aged, and the roof needed shingling. The inside was still functional, but less milking took place because modernization wasn't completed. There came a time when the barn was no longer needed. Only large dairy operations kept cows for milking. The neglected siding lost a few boards, and several shingles blew off in storms.

No one wanted to spend the money on upkeep until a grant helped pay for improvements. It has been listed on the historical registry through the work of my daughter-in-law, Mary. The whole family has fond memories of playing in the haymow, helping to clean the stalls, and playing with the many cats who make the barn their home, so all think it's a worthwhile project.

It's now a great-looking old barn again, unlike most around the area. Jed and Mary have kept it up on the outside, replacing some siding, giving it a fresh coat of paint and new shingles.

I often compare myself to that barn. I was so strong after Vietnam that I could lift those steel bars I used for welding with one hand. Without the constant workouts from the military, and my increasing age, I needed help from a hired man and later my sons to run the farm. My hairline began to recede, so I used a cap to cover the missing hair and keep my head warm. My body began to fade, especially when retirement gave me little to do.

Today, I again feel like the barn, all polished up on the outside, with new clothes purchased especially for the party, a recent haircut with my barber, and a close shave by the pretty young aide. However, I feel old and decrepit on the inside, unused for years and with no purpose here on earth.

The kids arrive to pick me up, the party goes smoothly, and I get to visit with many wonderful people who toast my numerous accomplishments.

Now I am sitting alone again in my room, waiting. My thoughts wander back to the one cool spring day, long ago in another old barn, revenge the only thing on my mind. Does living to show God's love make up for taking a life in the heat of the moment? Even when Jesus forgives, forgiveness of self is a hard-won battle. Has my one awful sin been blotted out? Can God's grace make a sinner whole?

Yes. I believe this to be true.

Janeen Swart is a teacher by profession, mother and grandmother by loving choice, and a secretary and gopher when needed. Having the goal of becoming a writer after retiring, Janeen took a Writing course at Indiana University NW. She also took two correspondence courses from The Institute of Children's Literature. Her first published book was through Lighthouse Christian Publishing, A Dog and His Boy. Later a YA book, The Hidden Truth was published by Soul Mate Publishing. Janeen also has several self-published books listed on Amazon.